D0961906

10/7

STRAY DOGS

STRAY DOGS

JOHN RIDLEY

Ballantine Books
New York

Copyright © 1997 by International Famous Players
Radio Picture Corporation

All rights reserved under International
and Pan-American Copyright Conventions. Published
in the United States by Ballantine Books, a division of Random
House, Inc., New York, and simultaneously in Canada
by Random House of Canada Limited, Toronto.

http://www.randomhouse.com

Library of Congress Cataloging-in-Publication Data
Ridley, John, 1965–
Stray dogs / John Ridley.—1st ed.
p.   cm.
ISBN 0-345-41345-8
I. Title.
PS3568.I3598S7   1997
813'.54—DC21   97-1414

Text design by Holly Johnson

Manufactured in the United States of America

First Edition: May 1997

10   9   8   7   6   5   4   3   2   1

To
Mom and Dad

To
Gayle, for her time

ACKNOWLEDGMENTS

Richard, Peter, Lori, Adam, Amy, Martin, and Emily.
Thank you.

"Fuck," was the invocation to prayer.

John prayed in earnest. "Jesus fucking Christ, c'mon!" It was a lonely imprecation of one to a higher power. God, Buddha, L. Ron Hubbard. Didn't matter. Right now it didn't fucking matter to John who ran the universe as long as he/she/it listened.

Here's the situation: an overheating Mustang in the middle of miles and miles of empty desert on a hotter-than-sin morning. You'd be praying, too.

"God fucking Christ! Come the fuck on!"

Oh, man. Check out what's lying up the road: the prayer's answer.

Through the shimmering heat and plume of steam that rose up from under the Mustang's hood, the gas station looked like a mirage. John prayed on to God, or Buddha, or L. Ron that it wasn't, because if it was—lost on a back road in a desert—he was dead. He'd be seeing God, or Buddha, or L. Ron in person, very soon.

It was real.

The Mustang rolled to the pumps, barely, the way an elephant just barely stumbles to its place of dying.

The station wasn't much: weather-beaten wood windows

1

long dusted over. A sign, paint faded, barely readable: HARLIN'S.

John worked the Mustang's hood, mindful of his bandaged left hand. A cloud of hot steam hit him full in the face.

"Goddammit!"

He went to the driver's side and gave a good lean on the horn.

Nothing.

He hit it again, long and hard.

A door fell open. A man shuffled out: skinny, overalls covered in grease, sweat-stained hat covering stringy hair. If white trash ever needed a poster child, this one got the job without much campaigning. "You want something?" He did a thing with his face that was either a squint or a smile, showing some crooked, blackened teeth. Those were the good ones.

"You Harlin?"

"Nope. Darrell."

"Harlin around?"

"He's up at the Lookout." A scrawny finger curled toward a plateau in the distance.

"Will he be back soon?"

"Nope. He's dead. The Lookout's a cemetery."

"You own this place?"

"Yep."

"Then why do you call it Harlin's?"

" 'Cause he used to own it."

"But he's dead."

"So?"

Darrell's eyes blinked in confusion. John could see his mind was working double time trying to sort things out.

John started to say something, but let it go. Instead:

2

"You want to take a look at my car? I think the radiator hose is—"

"Damn. Gonna be another hot one today." Darrell pulled out a rag and mopped his face. It left a streak of dirt that ran forehead to mouth. "That'll make five in a row. Never seen it so hot. Sometimes I don't even want to get out of bed. Just want to lay there and try to catch a breeze. I was in Mexico one time—"

Okay. Enough bullshit. "Look, pal." John's tone of voice spelled it out simple: I don't give a fuck about you, or your cracker-ass nonsense. "I've got someplace to be. You wanna just take a look at my radiator hose. It's busted."

Darrell's face twisted up like a scolded child's. He bent under the Mustang's hood and poked around at the engine. "It's your radiator hose. It's busted."

"I know it's busted. What did I just tell you?"

"Well, you know so damn much, why don't you just fix it yourself?"

"If I could, do you think I'd be standing here wasting my time? Can you fix it, or do I have to go somewhere else?"

"Somewhere else?" The idea of it gave Darrell a good laugh. "Mister, somewhere else is fifty miles from here. How you plannin' on getting there? You gonna push this heap yourself?"

"Okay, I'm stuck. You happy? Now, can you fix it or not?"

Darrell's lips parted in a crooked, blackened-tooth smile. It was the only smile he owned. He threw down the hood.

"Hey! Be careful."

"Yeah, I can fix it. Gotta run over to the yard and see if I can find a hose, or one close enough. Gonna take time."

3

"How long?"

"Time."

John's head dropped in frustration. "What time is it now?"

"Twenty after ten."

"Jesus. Twenty after ten and it must be ninety degrees already."

"Ninety-two. Only gonna get hotter. Two years ago we had this one week . . ."

John's bandaged hand went wiping across his forehead.

"What happened to your hand?"

"Accident."

"You got to be more careful. I remember this one time I—"

"Yeah, right. Someplace around here I can get a drink?"

"Truck stop up a piece. Not much, but it does the job."

"I'll be back. And be careful with her, will you?"

"It's just a car."

"It's not just a car. It's a 'sixty-four-and-a-half Mustang convertible." John grabbed up a backpack from the rear seat and slung it over his shoulder. "See, that's the difference between you and me, and why you live here and I'm just passing through."

John headed into town.

Darrell watched him go, then spat.

"**F**uck," again. But this time it wasn't a prayer. Just a dirty, angry word spat from John's lips.

The walk into town was maybe twenty minutes. Or maybe the burning sun made it seem that long. Either way it gave John time to consider his luck, of which he didn't have much. If he had he might be heading for San Diego, or Hawaii—what was the name of that girl he had fucked there?—instead of going back to Vegas.

Still, he was alive. Twice over, counting just making it to Harlin's. John rubbed at his bandaged hand. Days later, and it still hurt. Not the hand itself, but the memory of the pain had taken up permanent residence way down deep in his mind. John's eyelids dipped and he went over it: going on twenty of eleven now. Maybe an hour or so to get the Mustang fixed. Time enough to get something to eat and cool off. Back on the road, a few more hours to Vegas. Plenty of time. He had said by the end of the day, and the end of the day was more than twelve hours away.

Plenty of time, John, he told himself again in the kind of way you tell yourself things just to convince you they're true.

A pair of motorcycles rode by, kicking up a cloud of dirt and pebbles that rained down over John. He waved a hand in

5

front of his face, coughed, and swore after the riders. It was lost under the roar of the engines.

Check it: town, or what passed for it. A strip of store-fronts, post office/bus station, truck stop. With the wind behind him he could have spit across it. But it did have a truck stop, and a truck stop had beer, and that made this little shit hole just as big as it needed to be. John ran his tongue over his dry lips and headed for—

"Hey! You there!" Old man on the curb. Ragged clothes. Sunglasses. His skin was like tanned leather with wrinkles that looked hand-carved. A German shepherd lay next to him.

"You want something, old man?"

"Don't you call me old man. Ain't you got no respect?"

"You want something?"

"Yeah, I want something. I want you should run to that machine across the street and get me a pop." The old man wagged a finger at a soda machine that sat opposite from the post office/bus stop.

"You can't do it yourself?"

"Hell no, I can't do it myself. I'm blind. Can't you see that?"

"I'm sorry, I didn't—"

"What you think I was doing out here with these glasses on? Sunnin' myself?"

"I don't know. I thought you were keeping the light out of your eyes."

"I ain't got no eyes. You want to see?"

"Christ, no!"

"Lost them on Okinawa. Lost them fighting the war. Fought the war and lost my eyes just so you could come around here and make fun of me."

"I said I was sorry."

"Don't be sorry. Just be runnin' over there to get me a pop before I die of thirst."

"You got change?"

"Change? You want my change? I fought the war and lost my eyes just so I could give you my change?"

"All right, old man."

"I told you, don't call me old man."

"All right! Christ."

John went for the machine. He dug in his pocket for coins.

"Get me a Dr Peppa," the old man shouted after him. "I don't want no Pepsi. Pepsi ain't nothing but flavored water."

"Yeah. All right."

Two quarters through the slot. An old machine; a side door with bottles. John opened it, grabbed up a Dr Pepper, and headed back across the street.

"And don't forget to open it for me. I ain't trying to open my own bottles."

"Christ."

Back to the machine, then back across the street. The old man fumbled the bottle from John's hand. He took a deep swig, then paused to gasp. "That's what I needed." He held it up to John. "Want some?" A trail of saliva was strung between his mouth and the rim of the bottle.

"I'll pass." John squatted and stroked the old man's dog. "I think you'd better give your pooch a sip. He looks sick."

"That's 'cause he's dead."

John sprang back, falling into the middle of the street. "Oh, Jesus!"

"Hope you wasn't petting him, was you?"

"What the hell are you keeping a dead dog around for?"

7

"He's only just dead. What was I supposed to do with him? I can't take him away anywhere. And nobody wants to take him away *for* me. Do you?"

"Hell no!"

"See. Ain't nothing I can do but keep him here beside me. That's where he belongs anyways. Me and Sid, that's my dog, not anymore, but me and Sid been pals since after the war when I lost my eyes on Okinawa. . . ."

The old man's words tailed off into nothingness; a whisper a thousand miles away. Halfway down the street a woman, arms full of a long, awkward package, struggled toward a parked car. Real quick like that, the only thing in John's world was her.

The woman's hair was long, raven. It tumbled over caramel skin. Indi—Native Amer—Fuck the PC bullshit, John thought. She looked Indian. Maybe Mexican. The package made her toned muscles flex and define her arms. Cutoffs hugged her tight ass. A pair of dark nipples poked through a white T-shirt. Yeah, tits and ass and all that. Ten thousand years of evolution went into making this bundle. If she wasn't perfect, from where John was he couldn't see how.

He followed after.

The old man talked on to his dead dog.

Rolling up on her, casually: "Can I give you a hand, beautiful?" This close he could tell she was Native Ameri—Indian, and still perfect.

"I'm just going to my car." She didn't even bother to look at what John was selling. Cool as she is sexy.

"That's right on my way." John's head jerked over for a quick look at her backside. Even tighter at short distance.

"My mother told me never to accept offers from perfect strangers."

"Who's perfect?"

She stopped. She looked him over. Long, slow, like time came cheap to her.

A soft smile; friendly, harmless. "And my name is John. Now I'm not a stranger. See how easy it is for us to get to know each other, beautiful?"

"Do you have to call me that?"

"I don't know your real name."

"Maybe I don't want you to."

"Maybe. But if you didn't, I think you would have kept on walking."

"You're pretty full of yourself."

"My cup runneth over, beautiful." Still smiling. Still friendly. Still harmless.

She smiled back. "It's Grace."

"Can I carry your package for you, Grace?"

She hesitated, then hoisted the package into John's arms. The weight of it took him by surprise. He staggered. "Jesus."

"You sure you can manage?"

"I got it. It's just heavier than it looks." John shifted the load around in his bad hand.

"What happened to your hand?"

"Accident."

"You should be more careful. Want me to carry your pack for you?"

"No!" He jerked his shoulder and the pack away from Grace.

She stepped back.

John put up his smile. Friendly. Harmless. "Thanks. I've got it."

She smiled in return. They walked for her car.

Grace said, "It's very nice of you to help me. That package is kind of heavy, and it's so hot."

"No trouble. Really." John stopped at the trunk of a car. He lowered the package to the ground. The muscles in his back bit at him. "Wasn't nothing."

Embarrassed: "Oh, this isn't my car. It's down a ways. I should have parked closer. I just didn't think it would be so heavy. I could drive up."

Whipping out a little bravado: "That's all right. I've got it." John lifted the package. His back muscles got nasty about it. He sucked in a groan and followed Grace.

"It's just some new drapes and some curtain rods," she said. "If I had known it was going to be so much, I would have had them deliver it up at the house." Her voice was rich, full, sweet. She could read from a phone book and make it sound sexy.

John shifted his grip, trying to get a better hold. "It's nothing. Really."

"I just got tired of looking at the old drapes. Had them as long as I can remember."

"That a fact?" His back kept up its complaining. Now his arms had something to say about it.

"I saw these in the catalog and I just knew I had to have them. You ever seen something and knew you had to have it?"

"Yes, I have." The double entendre got lost in the strain of his voice. The heat, the weight, and the pain in his hand all tag-teamed to give John a good beating.

" 'Course they cost a little more than I should really be spending. But, what the hell? I don't hardly ever do anything nice for myself. You have to treat yourself every now and again."

"I . . . can't . . . argue. . . ." John's life flashed before him. It ended with him dead in the dirt under a pile of curtains.

Grace stopped at a Jeep. "This is it."

John couldn't talk his body into letting the package down easy. It hit the ground with a thud. Sweat sheeted him.

"Thank you, John."

"You're welcome"—a hard swallow—"Grace."

She looked at him, eyebrows twisted. "You're not from around here, are you?"

"What makes you say that? Just because I help a lady with her package?"

"You don't have that dead look in your eyes like the only thing you live for is to get through the day."

"I just drove in this morning."

Wide-eyed: "Drove into Sierra? What for?"

"Didn't have a choice. My car overheated up the road."

"Good luck it didn't happen a few miles back. Maybe they never would have found you. Day like today you'd be dead for sure."

"Yeah. My luck. I get to be stuck in this hole-in-the-desert."

"Least you can leave."

"Not until my car's fixed. I don't know how long that's going to take."

Grace stepped close. "And here I've made you all hot. . . ." Her hand went to his chest. It stroked away some of the sweat. "And wet."

John felt himself go hard.

"I could use some help carrying this box into the house. Not far. You could shower, get something cool to drink."

11

John tried to look like he was considering the offer. There wasn't much considering to do.

"Well, I could use something cool. . . ."

The Jeep tore across the open desert. No top. John rode with a hand up blocking the sun. He looked over at Grace, her hair swirling in the hot wind. The sun, the heat, didn't seem to bother her. She looked good against the barren canvas. She looked like she belonged here.

Casually, like maybe she was talking to herself: "Where are you coming from?"

"All over. Chicago, Miami, St. Louis. Just now Albuquerque."

"You get around."

"I guess I've got wander in my blood."

"Where you headed?"

"I don't know. I have to stop in Vegas. Then maybe I'll head to Santa Barbara. I might be able to pick up some work there."

"You just travel around, no direction, no steady work? You must like taking chances."

"If you're going to gamble, might as well play for high stakes."

"What happens when you lose?"

"I pack up, and go somewhere else."

Grace looked to John and smiled. Hers was not so friendly, not so harmless.

The smile faded. She said, "Somewhere else. I've never been anywhere else. Just once, years ago, the state fair. It was nice, but it wasn't nothing."

"I couldn't stay in a place like this. I wouldn't. Bore the shit out of me."

"So what would you do?"

"What do you mean, what would I do? I'd get the fuck out."

"What if you couldn't."

"Fuck couldn't. All you got to do is pick up, do whatever it takes, and get out. That's the part, though; whatever it takes. That's the key. You got to be able to do that: whatever it takes. If you can do that, then you're free."

The thought hung in the air for a split second. A jackrabbit darted into the road.

"Jesus Christ!" John's good hand braced the dash.

A tap to the brake. Grace jerked the wheel and the Jeep leaned hard around the rabbit. Smooth and in control. She put a foot back to the accelerator and drove on, mindless of the little event.

John looked back after the rabbit; a ball of fur springing into the sagebrush. "You see that?"

"Suicide."

"What?"

"They jump out like that 'cause they're trying to kill themselves."

"Why would a jackrabbit try to kill itself?"

She looked over. Dead eyes. "Boredom."

The house was more than John had expected; big, ranch-style. Santa Fe decor in and out. It looked as much a part of the desert as cactus. Expensive cactus. It was an oasis; a place to land away from the heat, and dirt and sweat and dryness. It was cool and clean and . . . safe. Yeah, that's what that feeling was. Safe. Here he didn't owe anybody anything, and nobody was trying to take anything from him. Not money, not . . . His hand started to hurt again, or at least the memory of it.

Grace poured John a glass of lemonade, led him to the master bedroom, then disappeared somewhere into the house. Occasionally John heard a sound; something moving, a laugh . . . ? Other than that, Grace ceased to exist; gone like a wet-dream fantasy driven away by the morning light.

He let his mind get comfortable in the thought of the house again. As much as he hated what he'd seen of this patch of dirt, as much as he couldn't stand the thought of being there just for the day, John figured he could get used to the house . . . to Grace. To Grace being in the house when he came home at night, or the middle of the day, or basically her just being there for him.

Yeah. John dug that idea. He slipped it on and walked

around in it for a while. A body like that, a place like this . . .
What's not to like?

He unwrapped his bandaged hand, stripped, went into
the bathroom. Turning on the shower, he stepped under it.
The water was cool, and it ran streaks of clean down his
dusted body. It should have relaxed him, but it only
reminded him of the rain. The rain reminded him of . . .
John's mind hit rewind.

Vegas was, is, about a lot of shit, but mostly it's about lights. Glowing, churning, beat-back-the-night kinds of lights. If something didn't come with neon, then it didn't really belong. Churches looked like discos, and discos looked like a Spielberg/LSD nightmare. The light was important. More important than the sunlight, 'cause the sunlight just showed you what an ugly city, in an ugly place, Vegas really was. The sunshine was like turning up the houselights at a nightclub and seeing the girl you've been trying to get drunk and fuck is just a beast with makeup spatulaed on.

The light was for the night. Bright colors. Quick motion. The light made it all look fun, and happy the way the lights on a carnival make you forget the Ferris wheel was put together that morning by some trailer trash who has a hard time deciphering the mysteries of a candy-bar wrapper. At night the light sucked you in, and the light showed the way, and the way was paved with greed and avarice and every other cheap human emotion that could be traded for a dollar—or less—in a back alley.

It's okay.

Vegas doesn't judge. Vegas just loves.

16

You want to blow some dough you should be spending on the house, or your kid's college fund. You go right ahead.

You want to get drunk with your middle-manager computer-salesmen buddies in town on convention from Dip-shit USA, then fuck some male prostitute 'cause he reminds you of that guy on the high-school swim team you had a crush on, but which, even to this day, you refuse to admit—not to yourself, or your wife, or your mistress. It's all cool. Vegas will forgive you in the morning. She's that kind of lover.

Do what you want. Be who you are. It's just babes, booze, and blackjack. Everything that's wrong with the world is right with Vegas.

John didn't look at the cards in his hand. To look at them was to think about them, and if he thought about them he might flinch, or smile, or he might try to look pissed like he didn't have the four kings that he had. But experienced poker players knew how to read a flinch, or a smile, and a pissed look is as good as saying: Jesus, am I holding on to some hot shit.

So John didn't look at his cards.

He rubbed his thumb over them, fanned out in his fingers, but he didn't look at the kings. He didn't think about them. He thought about the room he was sitting in. Dingy. Low-rent. The hotel was dingy and low-rent, too, but that was okay. These places, off the strip and in the heart of Vegas—not the touristy Vegas, but the places they don't print up in the brochures at the airport—these places were the place to gamble. Real action, high stakes. High risk, too, but that's what gambling was; risk. No risk, and you might as well be doing card tricks at some kid's bar mitzvah. Usually John figured things that way, but there's not much risk when you're nursing four kings.

But John didn't think about that.

He looked over at . . . what was her fucking name? Deana. Deandra. Push-up bra lifting her tits to the lip of her top. Hip-huggers. An ass John would eat cantaloupe out of, and he hated cantaloupe. A girl like that—a girl who knew where to find a good card game, fucked like a wild horse, and didn't care about getting held and stroked afterward, but just shut up and went right to sleep—a girl like that was almost perfect.

John thought about Gayle for a second. Was Deandra . . . Dina . . . was Dina worth tossing Gayle aside for? C'mon, man. What kind of stupid-ass question is that?

Three other players at the table. A fat guy, a faggoty guy, and some Italian guy. Check out that silk suit this dago's got on. Christ, it's like he's planning on catching Frankie and the rest of the Pack for the late show at the Sands.

Fucking Vegas, John said to himself with a smile. It brings them all out.

The bet was to the Italian, and he went out. The faggoty guy followed. No surprise there. The pot was getting hot, and let's face it: Those kind don't have the balls to hang tough. Not like Johnny. Johnny had the balls of four kings swinging between his legs. It was just him and the fat guy now, and the fat guy was going down.

John slid a pile of chips forward. Three thousand. Fat man drops, John's got the pot. Fat man raises, John goes home with swollen pockets. He got a rhythm going in his head: Don't smile, don't smile, don't smile.

Fat man gave the whole thing some serious thought. In, or out? Fold, or stay?

Fat man stayed, and he stayed in a very big way. All in

with his chips, then his blimplike fingers floated inside his jacket and pulled out a wad of cash that bulged like the gelatinous area around his waist. Fatty started flipping bills down into the pot, one after the other after the other. Leaves in fall, that's the way they rained down. They didn't stop raining until they had pushed the pot upward twenty thousand.

The five little blimps floated what was left of the cash wad back into Fatty's pocket. Fatty didn't say or do anything. He gave away nothing; was it a bluff, or was he for real? Fat Man reached over to a cream puff and wedged it into his mouth. Such a tiny mouth for such a big guy.

Here's how it was: John couldn't cover the bet. If he couldn't cover the bet, he would have to fold. If he folded he walked away from a sure score, then he would've showed up to the party and blown a handful of hours just to get a stick in the ass for his trouble. He felt something creep across his forehead: Sweat. "I . . . I can't cover the bet."

Even at that the Fat Man gave nothing away.

"I, uh, I don't have enough money—"

"I'll cover you," the Italian mumbled.

He hadn't spoken as much as a word to John all evening, so this caught him by surprise. "Wha . . . ?"

"You want to stay in, I'll cover you."

"I—"

"It ain't charity, okay. I cover you, you win, you owe me the cover plus thirty percent."

This hit John sideways. "You want in on my winnings?"

The silk suit shrugged with the Italian's shoulders. "You want to stay, you want to drop, I don't care. But you drop, you get nothing."

John chewed at his lip like he was trying to pull loose

an answer. It was fucking stupid: Take someone else's cover just so they can ride off with part of your winnings. It was fucking—

A hand rode over John's shoulders. It was . . . Dana . . . ? Just standing there looking good. She was that kind of woman: the kind who could get things done without moving a muscle. But she did move. Her tit rubbed up against the back of John's neck.

He looked down at the four badass fellas in his hand standing shoulder to shoulder.

Still, all that wasn't enough. "I don't know if I should—"

What's that? Across the table: He's laughing. The fucking faggot is laughing. Oh no he didn't. John could take a lot of shit, a whole lot of shit. He's that kind of guy where shit raining down on him didn't mean much. You get that way when it's been raining shit all your life. But what he couldn't stomach is some guy who takes it up the ass for a living laughing at him.

"I'm in." Just like that. "I'm in."

The Italian nodded.

John called. With no fanfare he laid out his boys.

Fat Man put down his cards.

John took a quick trip around the universe. More than one, in fact. He went swimming in deep darkness where even stars didn't shine. A few years later he floated back to that dingy, little hotel where no tourist dare tread. He floated back into the room that was some orange-brown hideousness. He hovered over a pathetic, little man who looked like he wanted to cry. Then he realized he was hovering over himself. John was having one of those *X-Files* out-of-body experiences, like people who were dying.

Only John wasn't dying.

He could hope it and wish it, but he still had some ugly living to do. No putting it off, boy. Time to get back in that sack a' flesh and get on with the nasty business of being you.

Real time picked up again from the instant that had slapped John into oblivion and back: Fatty had just laid down his cards. Fatty had just laid down a three and four aces.

"How about that?" Fatty said.

The queer laughed.

The wop nodded.

Yeah. How fucking about that? One guy gets four kings, which is so nearly goddamn impossible to do in the first place, and which is so more nearly goddamn impossible to top. But some guy, at that very table, not only beats him, but he beats him clean with four aces.

"How about that?" John repeated to no one in particular, but sort of to . . . Denise.

Denise, or whatever her name is, had nothing to say to that. She had nothing to say 'cause she wasn't there anymore. Not right there. Not right next to him. She had floated across the room over by the Italian, where she hung off his shoulder and smiled an "oh you silly boy" smile at John.

The girl.

The girl who rubbed up against him when he was winning at poker at the Flamingo. The girl who knew where to find a game with some real action. The Italian who didn't know John from Hitler, but offered to cover his bet. The Fat Man with his four aces.

A moment of clarity hit John the way a truck hits a cat too stupid to get out of the road. "You set me up. You little cunt."

"No need for that." The Italian jumped in like all of a

sudden he got manners. "You ain't got to talk to her like that."

"Yeah, I'm talking to your girl, aren't I? She's yours. The fat guy's yours. You fucking the fag, too?"

The fag stopped laughing. Nobody said anything, most of all John. He wasn't a tough guy. Never had been. And now was a bad time to pick it up as a hobby.

Seconds strolled by. Then the Italian worked up something like a smile. "That what you think; this is a shake-down? That what you thinking?"

"Yeah, that's what I'm thinking. You float that bitch's ass around town every other night—"

"Hey, I told you about that."

"She suckers guys like me down here, you let us get it in our heads we can do a little winning, then as soon as we stick our balls out you cut 'em off. Fifteen, twenty thousand a head. That's a real nice racket you got. Real good. I guess that's all that's left for cheap hoods like you now that Dino and Sammy are gone."

Sure. Not a time to act tough, but it felt good.

The Italian just smiled. There was nothing friendly, or happy, or warm about it. He just smiled. When he was through smiling he said: "Maybe you like to think that. Maybe it makes losing easier to a punk like you when you get it in your head the whole world's against you. That the bunch of us got together, picked you out of the millions 'cause you're so goddamn special we couldn't take our eyes off of you, and then we rode you like a pony. That make you feel okay with everything?

"Or let's try it another way: Let's try it you're just a little wise-ass kid who rolls into town—my town—with faded dungarees and a full head of hair thinking he's bulletproof; thinking he can fight with the big dogs and not get bit. Only you can't. Only you're not that good. Only you know as much about cards as a priest does about fucking. That's how I see things."

The Italian rubbed at his pinky ring; big and shiny and tacky the way pinky rings are. "But when you get down to it, when you really look at it, it don't matter. It don't matter if we made you, or you just landed your sorry self here on your own. You lost, and you owe, and I want my money."

John tried to stare the Italian down. Sweat rolled into his eye, and he flinched. "I . . . It's, like, I don't have the money here."

"Like?"

"If I did I wouldn't have needed you to—"

"But you have it."

"What's tha—"

"The money. You have the money. You wouldn't take a bet you couldn't cover."

"No. I mean, no I wouldn't take a bet I—"

"You want to write a check? I'll take a check. I'm sure you're good for it. Make it out to Mr. Vesci."

"I can't write a check. I have to—"

There. Across the table: that fucking fag with his fucking fag laugh. If John had two seconds alone he'd—

The Italian broke the train of thought. "So you have the money? You have cash money?"

". . . Yes."

Like it was the most obvious thing in the world: "Then get it."

Somehow John got to his feet. Somehow he started for the door.

"Oh, hey." The Italian's voice came after him. "I don't

feel like looking for people tonight. It's going to rain, and I'm not trying to go around looking for people in the rain, see how I'm saying?"

John started to say something when the girl shifted around to the fag. She kissed him. She looked dead at John, but she kissed the fag full and deep and hard on the lips. The fag kissed her full and deep and hard back. Like maybe he wasn't a fag. Or maybe he was, and this was the girl's way of saying to John she'd give it to a queer before she gave it to him.

Didn't matter.

She was trying to put the hurt on, and she did.

John left.

It was starting to rain.

The drive home, the drive to Paradise Road was quick. Even with the rain it was quick. But it was just long enough for panic to get the kind of grip on John that a man couldn't shake loose.

He should have known better, was the song playing over and over in his head. The girl, the setup; all the neon in town couldn't have made things any plainer. And it wasn't the first time he'd gotten suckered like this. The last time he'd barely gotten away without having his heart carved from his chest. The last time he was lucky enough to hook up with a couple of people who knew how to get a guy out of a jam. A thought came to him about calling them again.

Yeah, like they'd want to stick their necks out for John one more time. Besides, Brice had split to L.A., and Ned and Jude . . . weren't they dead?

Around a corner. Into the driveway. John flew out of

the car into his house. Gayle's house, really, but he called it his since he split the rent. A few times. Well, split, but not right down the middle.

Inside. Gayle sitting there like she'd been waiting for him.

John didn't have time for a lot of words, so he didn't bother with many. "How much money you got?" There wasn't room for debate either, so he skipped over that, too. "I'll pay you back first time I can, but I need money. All you can give me."

Gayle just sat there. Didn't move. Didn't say a word. Just sat.

The panic bit at John harder, so he spit things at her again. "I need money." To color things nice he tossed in "Baby."

Gayle sat some more. Mountains should be so still. Eventually: "It's our anniversary."

John tried to ask "What?" but all that came out of him was empty air. Everything slowed down for a beat. John looked at Gayle. At her legs that stretched out from the skirt she wore when she waitressed at the hotel downtown, the one where he had first met her. She had good legs. Not spindly little runway-model things that looked like they'd snap in a heavy breeze. She had strong, lean, powerful legs. Great legs. Great for a woman her age, although John wasn't exactly sure how old Gayle was. She was Asian, and Asian chicks always—usually—looked younger than they were. Still, those legs were too tight for an old girl. But she had gray in her hair. Streaks, like little silver rivers that flowed through a rich, black terrain. So John figured things two ways: He figured Gayle was either an older woman God graced with two of the best lower appendages mankind had ever witnessed, or she was a kid who bled gray streaks for whatever reason. Either way it made for a nice package and a good fantasy, and John wasn't about to spoil it asking for specifics.

Gayle brought John back around. "It's our anniversary, and you kept me here waiting."

A "what the fuck are you talking about" look got all up on John's face. He said to Gayle, "What the fuck are you talking about?"

"Eight months. It's been eight months since our first date."

Is that what she was talking about? He had some *Ocean's Eleven* wannabe wanting thirteen large, or his body on a slab, and she was talking nonsense. "Didn't you hear me? I've got guys who want—"

"Didn't you hear me? Eight months today. Tonight. Eight months since our first date, and you left me here waiting all night."

As tenacious as the panic was, even it had to take a backseat to bullshit. Don't matter if you're king of England, or a street bum. If you're in a relationship, women have a way of slapping you with crazy, far-out, swinging shit that can knock everything else from your mind. It's enough to make a guy quit women; send a straight one into another man's ever-loving arms.

"It's not eight months tonight."

"It is."

"It isn't. I came to Vegas a year ago, and I met you the first week I was in town."

"I know that. Don't you think I know that? I'm not crazy. It's not the anniversary of the first time we met. It's the anniversary of the first time we went out."

John thought about the fag he'd left behind at the card game. He thought: All right, you know what? Maybe being gay isn't such a bad thing. Gay boys probably make for real happy couples. Just two guys together, doing what men do, understanding men. They're happy. Sure they're happy. That's why they call them gay.

But for now, he had a woman to deal with. "The first ti . . . Gayle, I need money. I'm not trying to talk about when we met, or when we . . ." John sputtered, then got back to it. "I need money!"

A look got in Gayle's eyes. It was a look that asked questions beyond a boyfriend rushing in from the rain screaming for dough. It was the look chicks get when they know something's up, and chicks always know when something's up. That's their way. That's their nature. That's what they do.

Gayle stepped to John.

Against himself John took half a step back, but that's how determined she moved.

Gayle closed her eyes for a moment. Just a moment. When she opened them they burned with a fire from hell. "You were with a woman."

"Wha . . . I . . . What are you . . . ?" John went through all the classic busted-guy moves. Fumphering, rolling his eyes, adopting the sudden inability to comprehend the spoken language. That's their way. That's their nature. That's what guys do.

"I can smell her on you, John, and she smells cheap. She smells like a two-dollar whore who takes coupons."

"I . . . why are you—"

"Admit it. Admit you were with a woman!"

The money, boy. Get things back around to the money.

Just admit it, and get back to the dough. "Yeah, okay, I saw a girl tonight, but it—"

"Our anniversary, and you were with another woman?"

"It's not our . . . all right, it's our anniversary, but our first date? What is that? That's bullshit. That's a bullshit anniversary."

"Not to me!" The veins in Gayle's eyes flushed. Soon they'd get wet, then would come the crying. The goddamn crying.

John tried to slog on. "Eight months. It's not even a year. I could understand a year. Gayle, the woman . . . I was at a card game. I was at a game, and she was there. That's what I'm trying to talk about; the card game. I lost, I lost big, and I lost to the wrong people. I need dough, and I . . . For Christ's sake, I need money!"

"Any other night and I think I could have gotten past this. But tonight . . . ? Another woman on our anniversary?"

The truth. This is what telling the truth got him. Truth brings only pain, and heartache, and difficulty. If you care about someone, if you love them, and if you want to spare yourself a little suffering at the same time, then truth has got no place in a relationship and should only be used when a good lie doesn't come quick enough.

Gayle went into a very controlled breakdown; a strong woman getting weak. Even for John, even for a guy who would trade his soul in a back-alley pawnshop for roulette money, this was hurtful to watch. "I can't take it, John. Eight months I invested in you just so you could go blow it on the first piece of ass that caught your eye. I'm too old for that. I gave you my time, and I don't have time to give. Eight months I could have put into finding a guy who's maybe not the best looking, or the sharpest, but a guy who gives a fuck about me. That's not much, is it? That's not any more than anyone else is looking for: At the end of the day, when you're beat like a horse, there's someone—somewhere—who gives a fuck about you."

"Gayle, I—"

The second John started up, Gayle slapped him down with her voice. "I WANT THINGS IN LIFE, TOO! Is that so hard to believe that anybody besides you should have needs? You want some other girl, go get some other girl, but not on my time. Not on my clock."

Silence came on hard. It came, and it stayed. When John spoke, even in a whisper, his voice clapped like thunder. "I'm sorry, Gayle. I'm really, really sorry for what I did. And I would do anything I could to make it up to you. Anything. But right now I need your help. If you don't help me . . . I'm in real trouble, Gayle. Serious trouble." A beat, then for added push: "Please."

Gayle didn't even have to put thought to it. "I have about twenty-two thousand in my savings account."

"Oh, God, thank you, sweetie. I only need thirteen grand. And I'm going to pay you back. I swear, I'm going to—"

"You can't have it."

Real quick John forgot how to speak.

"Not a dime. You can't have any of it."

John struggled hard as he learned to talk again. ". . . Don't you . . . ? Listen to me: I owe people. They are going to hurt me, Gayle. They are going to hurt me very badly if I don't pay them. You have to help me."

Nothing.

"Goddammit, they're going to kill me, Gayle! I NEED MONEY!"

Something: Gayle's lips got with a slight smile. Yeah,

they were going to kill John, and she was digging every second of it. Hell hath no fury . . .

The ground started to twist and sway under John's feet. The world got that way for him real quick like; twisty, turny, and out of control. He was in a spiral that was going to take him straight into the ground at two hundred miles per hour, and leave nothing but a burned-out crater.

As he started his flight down John took one last look around. The only thing he saw was Gayle. Still smiling.

In Vegas, night was not much different than day, or at least evening. There was light. Always light. And the darkness offered little cover. Even with all the people, the rain, Fremont Street was no place to try and hide.

John was trying it.

What had happened was he had gathered up everything he owned—every knickknack, every doodad, every whatchamacallit—and hauled ass down to a pawnshop, which, next to the casinos, was the best business going in Vegas.

Eight hundred dollars. He brought all his stuff in, dumped it on a counter, and all it added up to was eight hundred dollars. That's the essence of a man right there: when push comes to shove how much cash he can turn his life into. Eight hundred wasn't enough to get John buried good.

So he didn't sell his stuff. He held on to it, like somehow he was holding on to his pride. All he was holding on to was eight hundred dollars' worth of junk.

The only thing for him to do was split town. When he headed back to his Mustang there was a big goon-looking guy hovering over it. Maybe it was a big goon guy who dug Mustangs.

Maybe.

But it was more likely he was a big goon who did collecting for cats like this Mr. Vesci. And since John wasn't in a hurry to find out what kind of goon it was, he opted for beating it the hell out of there fast as he could.

So here he was, now, running up and down Fremont. If he made it to Union Plaza he could hop a train and . . . But then he'd have to leave the Mustang. There ain't no leaving the Mustang. Okay, so he'd hide out a bit, then double back—

Shit! Check that out: another goon. Or is it the same one? Or is John just getting paranoid?

Naw, this dude is definitely following him.

A plan went on heavy rotation in John's head: Shake the goon, get the Mustang, get out of town. It wasn't much of a plan. Real simple, but it would work.

Maybe.

If he got past the first part.

Maybe.

John cut down an alley. That was a fucking mistake. It was a dead end. Panic started biting at him again. John spun and headed for the street. As he reached the mouth of the alley something hit him across the chest. It could have been a brick, or a lead pipe. It was a fist. The blow sent him flying back the way he came.

A giant's hands—the goon—lifted him by the shoulders and slammed him against the alley wall. The air shot from John's lungs. He gasped for a second, then caught a deep breath, sucking in a mouthful of rainwater with it. His own voice kept screaming in his head, scolding him: You shouldn't have run. You shouldn't have run.

Like that was the only thing he shouldn't have done.

Another voice: "I want my money."

John tried to move. His wrist was held against the wall tight. Tighter. His fingers spread and clutched brick. He felt like he was about two seconds from his hand popping off his arm.

Again the voice: "I want my money."

A sound; metal scraping metal. John could see the switchblade through the corner of his eyes. Then it was gone. Then his fingers burned white-hot. He screamed. The night went pitch-black. That's a hell of a thing to happen in Vegas.

One more time as the world faded away: "I want my money."

With his right hand John wiped the water from his face. He looked over at his left hand pressed against the shower tile. A streak of red water ran from what was left of his pinky and ring finger.

Grace's bedroom. John toweled off, pulled on his jeans. He snatched up his shirt off his backpack, went to a mirror, and with his rebandaged hand, did his best to fumble the buttons closed.

In the mirror he saw Grace watching by the doorway. He slowed his dressing, puffed up a little, gave her something to look at. She entered, having changed into a sundress, carrying a glass of lemonade.

"Thought you might like a refill."

John took the glass, drank it down. He ran an ice cube across his forehead. "That's good. Thanks."

"You're welcome." Grace sat on the edge of the bed. Legs apart.

John said, "I guess it must get kind of lonely for a woman living in a big house by herself."

"I guess it would."

"What do you do anyway?"

"Little of this, little of that. Mostly I tell fortunes."

"Where'd you pick that up?"

"From my father. He was the tribal shaman."

"A medicine man?"

"Those are white words, not ours."

John shrugged. "Nice house for a shaman's daughter. You must be pretty good."

Grace leaned forward. The top of her dress fell open offering up a real nice view of her real nice tits. "Come here."

John went to her. He went down on one knee, and she gently cupped his head in her hands. John felt his penis stretch and press against the inside of his jeans.

"There is something in your past," Grace said. But not Grace. It was like ... another voice. Deeper than hers. Darker. John caught a little shiver, just a little one, like someone was walking on his grave.

Grace went on: "There is something you want to keep hidden. There is a pain. Something—no, someone you cannot forget. And there is something you want very badly. It seems very far away to you, but you are determined, and you will do what you must to get it."

John pulled away from her. Fortune-teller or not, Grace cut a little too close.

"My face tell you all that?"

"It tells me what every face tells me. Everybody has a past. They have a pain and they have something they want." She dropped her head and looked up at him through a river of her hair. "What do you want, John?"

His eyes fell over her, big and slow. He started to sweat. "The same thing you want."

"Really?" The tip of her tongue darted between her lips. "I want to hang drapes."

She brushed past him out of the room. John took an ice cube from the glass and bit down on it hard.

Grace stretched up on the top of a stepladder. "Hold me."

John gingerly laid his hand on her waist.

"Tighter."

He held her tighter.

She hung drapes.

He stared at her ass.

"All done. Lift me down."

"What?"

"Lift me down."

He hoisted her up and off the stepladder to the ground. They stood for a moment, quiet, his hands still on her.

"You can let go of me now. I'm safe."

Reluctantly, John's hands dropped away. Grace stepped back from the windows.

"How do they look?"

"Like you."

"Beautiful?"

"Like they're made of polyester."

It was meant to be a joke, but Grace gave John a hard look like she didn't get it. Or she didn't like it.

She said: "I like them. I was sick of looking at this room. I think they add a little life."

"Nothing like a little liveliness."

"No more drapes to hang. Now what should we do?" The question was loaded as full as it would go.

"I have ideas."

"Such as?"

John took Grace by the shoulders. He drew her in and kissed her. Warm, passionate, endless. She didn't kiss back. A dead fish would have given him more.

"All right, Grace. No more games."

Innocently: "Games?"

"You flirt with me, then run cold. You lead me on, then slap me down. I don't go for being jerked around."

"Oh, really? And what game did you want to play? 'Carry my box, and I just fall into bed with you'?"

Enough is enough. Every man has a breaking point and John, finally, hit his. He went for the door, dipping slightly to grab up his pack from the floor. "I think I can find my own way back to town."

"Maybe I like to learn something about a man first. Maybe I like to know what he's made of."

John stopped. He turned until he faced Grace. "I'm flesh and blood. That and a few memories of bad women. Just like most guys. But you already know that. You read my fortune." Lips twisted like he wanted to spit: "Thanks for the lemonade." He made for the door.

"You never did answer my question."

Without looking back: "Still playing games?"

"That's not an answer. What is it you want?"

"You know what I want."

"Maybe I just want to hear you say it."

He faced her. Across the room Grace's breath came quick, her lips parted. The pack slid from John's shoulder.

He moved. He went toward her fast, hard, determined; speed gathering like an animal ready to strike. She closed her eyes, arched her back. She let him come. She was ready to be taken.

"Grace!"

The voice came down like a brick wall, stopping John dead. He sucked in a breath, rustled up whatever composure he could, turned. . . . Behind him was an older man. Only the gray woven in his black hair hinted it. Tree trunks for legs, barrel-chested, arms like a steelworker who wrestled bulls on the weekend.

"Jake," Grace said. "I thought you would be at work." If she was giving the time of day, she couldn't have been more casual.

Jake said: "Who the 'ell is this?" Wolves growled less.

"Who the hell are you?"

"Guess."

It didn't take John much figuring. "Her husband?"

"Bright boy." Irish brogue as thick and hard as the rest of him. "Now, who are you, and what the 'ell are you doing 'ere? And it better sound right, or God help me I'll break ya in half."

Voice steady: "I was helping your wife. I met her in town. She needed a hand with her drapes." John swallowed. "That's all."

"Sure at that. Didn't much look like you were hanging drapes."

"I swear to you that's all that happened. I haven't so much as set foot in your bedroom."

Something like a laugh came out of Jake. "A lot that means."

"Grace, tell him."

She picked up a glass of lemonade and sipped it incidentally.

"Dammit, Grace! Tell him!"

Coy: "If he says that's what happened, Jake, it must be true."

A fire lit under Jake. "I've half a mind to—"

Whatever Jake had to say, that's not where John was. He was on Grace. "Is that what this is all about? You sucker me out here so you can watch the two of us beat the shit out of each other over you?"

John's right hand curled into a fist. His nails bit into his palm. Something flashed in his mind: him and Grace and violence. He uncurled his hand.

"Forget it," he said. To Jake: "You want to take my head off, I won't even try to stop you. I deserve it for being stupid. But if you don't, then I think I'd like to be on my way."

A long moment. Very long. Everyone waited for something to happen.

Nothing did.

Jake stepped from the door.

John picked up his pack and left.

Grace sipped her lemonade.

On a cool summer's evening, with a breeze before you, the walk from Grace's—Grace and Jake's—back into town was probably not much more than a forty-five-minute stroll. Long, but not hard.

But mid-morning, in the sweltering heat, it was like walking through hell with gasoline shorts on.

John stumbled along under the sun, shirt dark with sweat and sporting a fresh coat of dust. This, he thought—and he had plenty of time for it—is where listening to his dick got him.

"Dammit," mumbled from his lips.

The strap of the backpack bit into his shoulder. It was heavy with something besides its own weight, heavy with iniquity. The thing about gamblers is they make very good bookkeepers since they've got a head for numbers. The other thing about them, as the partners of Lewis and Associates would discover come Monday when they opened their offices and found their gutted safe, is that gamblers are unreliable. Don't hire them in the first place, and for God's sake when they up and quit and move to Vegas to be closer to the needle of their habit, be sure to get the office keys back from them.

John felt bad. Not for stealing, but for making it harder for the next down-and-out dicer to rip someone off in a moment of desperation.

A Cadillac came up from behind and slowed at John's side. The window slid down. Jake was driving.

"Get in, lad. I'll give you a lift."

John didn't move.

"Pushing a hundred degrees. Too hot to be walking. Few minutes of this'll drive you crazy, sure."

John still didn't move. Through the window he felt the cool of the Caddy's air conditioner. He looked around; nothing, no one. A man could kill another out here, and not a soul would ever know about it.

"Come on and get in, fer frig sake. If I was going to give you trouble, I'd 'ave done it already."

The potential to get himself killed versus air-conditioning. John took air-conditioning. He got in the Caddy, resting his bandaged hand on the dash.

"What happened to yer hand?"

"Accident."

"Ya got to be—"

"Yeah, I know. More careful."

They rode awhile in silence, then:

"I guess we've never been properly introduced. Jake McKenna."

John tried it out. "Jake McKenna. That's a solid name."

"I'm a solid man."

"John Stewart."

"What brings you to Sierra, Mr. Stewart?"

"Bad luck. My car overheated. I pulled in to have it fixed."

"Where you headed?"

"Vegas. Then California. Santa Barbara."

"You live there?"

"Got work. I know a man has a boat. Wants me to sail it for him."

"Sure, and yer a sailor man? That'd be the life." Jake's eyes drifted like he was watching a movie in his head. "Drive cross-country to California, step on a boat, and just sail away. You could pretty well disappear like that. Aye, just sail away until everything you were was just a memory." The movie ended and Jake came back. "I guess a little place like this would just be a dot on a map to you after a while."

"I hope so." John shifted uncomfortably. "Listen, Mr. McKenna, about your wife: If I had known she was married—"

"It wouldn't 'ave made any difference to you, now, would it? Not a whit. Sure, and ya know why? Yer a man's got no scruples."

"Wait a second—"

"Ah, I can smell it on you."

Jake's hand shot out and wiped the back of John's neck. He held his fingers to his nose.

"Aye, that's the sweat of a man who 'asn't got an honest bone in his body. Don't take offense, lad. A man's got no ethics is a free man; a man who can do as he pleases. I envy you that. 'Sides, I can hardly hold anything agin' you. That Grace is a cheeky one, and she's got a body to match, eh?"

Jake gave an elbow to John.

John smiled, but not too much. Play with Jake, sure, but for Christ's sake don't piss him off.

"Eh? She is at that. I knew when I married her she was a free spirit. A woman with her looks, and a man my age?

41

What was I to expect 'cept that she would play around some. But you see something like that in a town like this and you don't think. You just do. So I married her. And that's where I am. What are you to do, eh? Women . . ."

"You can't live with them. You can't get them to dress up in a Nazi outfit and lap dance for you."

Jake barked a laugh. "That Grace made ya pretty hot, didn't she?"

John held back for a second, then: "Yeah."

"Taking you up to the house with that smile of hers. Bet she wiggled her arse in front of you more than once. Then me busting in like some wild bear. Bet that got yer fire stoked."

The fire started to come back. "Like you don't know."

"Mad like a dog in heat. I can tell you got a temper."

John gave a little laugh.

"Bet you just wanted to snap her neck right there, didn't you. Bet you just wanted to kill her."

John's laugh went full and hearty. Jake joined in, then stopped.

"Would you?"

"Would I what?"

"Would you kill her?"

John's laugh came again. He laughed alone.

"I asked you a question, lad."

"Why would I kill your wife?"

"For me. 'Cause I'm tired of her, and her little games. Because you could do it and drift away on yer boat and no one would ever see ya again. Because I've a fifty-thousand-dollar insurance policy out on her, and I'd be more than happy to give the man who does away with Grace a good chunk of it."

42

John stared out the windshield at the desert, at nothing. He came back to an old thought; a man could kill someone out here, and no one would ever know about it.

"I'm not a murderer, Mr. McKenna."

"How do you know if you've never tried?"

"This is a joke, right? You just want to rattle me a little. Right?"

They reached town. Jake eased the Caddy to the side of the road. He looked to John, all smiles. "That's right. Nothing but a joke. That's all."

John got out of the car. No good-byes, no words exchanged. Jake pulled away. For a long moment John looked after him.

"This fucking town is crazy."

The store was at the outer edge of town. Dark. Shabby. Empty. The old Mexican woman behind the counter watched John as he circled a rack of snack food before snatching up a pack of Twinkies. He dropped them on the counter in front of her.

"Got any cold soda to go with that?"

The old woman put a finger to her ear. "Eh?"

"Cold soda. You got any cold soda?"

"Slowly, *por favor. Mi inglés no está bueno.*"

"Soda. You know."

John cupped his hand and made like he was drinking.

"Oh, something to eat. *Sí.*" She picked up the Twinkies and smiled, happy like a kid who just learned to add numbers.

"Not eat. Drink. What the fuck is 'drink' in Spanish? Uh . . . *agua?*"

The old woman's eyes went wide. Her mouth stretched in a silent scream.

"What? What did I say? I didn't mean it! I don't know Spanish!"

From behind John came a click. He turned to stare into the big, black eye of a Glock 17 automatic pistol. John didn't know it as a Glock 17 automatic pistol. All he could see was the big, black eye. A biker in black leather held it—the gun—in an outstretched arm. Another biker, dressed alike, stood behind the first at the door with the shade pulled, watching the street. John and the black eye just kept staring at each other.

The biker, the one with the gun, said, "That's right, lady. Keep it in you and nobody gets dead. That goes for you, too, stud. Gimme the money. Now!"

"Eh," the old woman crackled.

"The *dinero*, señora," said the biker at the door. "Hand it over."

John shifted his weight, trying to angle his pack from the biker.

The black eye kept watching.

The old woman rang open the cash register. The biker with the gun pawed at it. He held up the take for his partner's approval.

"That's it? Lady, I got kids to put through school."

"Es all I have."

To John: "Your wallet. Let's have it."

John slid his wallet from his hip pocket and dropped it on the counter.

The biker scooped it up. The black eye swung back and forth between the old woman and John as the biker backed toward the door. The eye stopped and took a good, long look at John.

The biker said, "Toss me the pack."

"There's nothing in it. Just books."

"I'm a reader. Toss it."

A word choked and gargled in John's throat, then finally crawled out of his mouth. "No."

"No?"

The black eye floated closer.

"Señor, give it to him."

"That's all right, *chiquita*," the biker said, nice-guy sweet. "He doesn't want to give me the pack. . . ."

The barrel of the gun tapped lightly against John's temple. He flinched.

"He doesn't have to give me the pack."

Again, the light tap; metal to flesh. John shut his eyes as if that alone could stop the coming bullet.

The old woman's face flooded with terror.

The biker jerked the gun back, then forward. It whistled through the air and crunched against John's skull. Fireworks went off behind his eyes. He bounced against the counter and saw the floor rushing toward him. He lay there, arms and legs flailing, like a stepped-on bug.

The old lady screamed.

"Fuck, man," the biker at the door yelled over her. "Let's get out of here!"

The biker with the gun snatched up the pack. He looked at the old woman, hands to her mouth; her finger, a diamond ring. He grabbed for it.

"No," she wailed.

"Fuck that!" He tore the jewelry from her.

She cried out again in a wild piercing shriek.

The biker at the door: "Christ, let's go!"

The other biker held up the ring. A piece of flesh hung from it. "Now we go."

He jammed the ring in a pocket, slung John's pack over his shoulder, and turned for the door.

The old woman's hands went under the counter. "You go. You go to *el diablo*!"

A click, a roar, a flash of fire from a shotgun blast. The

pack exploded. The biker flipped forward like he just got smacked in the back by the hand of God. His body thudded against the ground under a shower of blood and shredded money.

"Nooooo," John wailed.

The second biker froze. "Oh, shit! Oh, shit! Oh, shit!"

The old woman pumped the shotgun, fired as the biker dove out the door. The buckshot ripped apart the wooden frame where his head had been.

John stumbled to the dead biker. Blood gurgled from a hole in his back that was punched through what was left of the pack. Everything was a mushy, soggy black red. If there was any money left, John couldn't tell it from body parts.

His lip quivered. His bandaged hand began to throb. "No," he muttered, all pathetic. "No."

"Señor." The old woman came up behind him. "Señor, are you all right?"

John pressed a hand to his bleeding head and mumbled something.

"I call the *policía*."

"No!" He made the long climb to his feet and staggered when he got there. "No police."

"But, señor—"

"No police. After I'm gone."

He started the journey toward the door, the floor slipping and sliding under his woozy legs.

"Señor. You need a doctor."

The door. A moment's rest. "No police!"

John headed outside. The sun and the heat were waiting for him.

John walked. He didn't know where he was going, but in a town this small he figured sooner or later he would end up somewhere he needed to be. Needles were jammed into the gash on his head, and phantom pain had his missing fingers in a vise grip. John wanted to vomit, but to vomit you have to eat, and he hadn't swallowed food for what seemed like more than a day.

A thought came to him. One so obvious now that he didn't know how he could have missed it before: He was in hell. It was the only explanation. His car breaking down just where it happened to. Meeting a woman like Grace—crazy—and her husband—crazier. The bikers, the Spanish woman with the shotgun, the shredded money, and the heat. The never-ending heat. This was too much far-out, crazy shit for one day, let alone one morning. This was hell.

Except that John was bleeding, and blood seemed a little too mundane for eternal damnation. So it wasn't hell, just an incredible simulation.

After a while John ended up at Harlin's, the Mustang parked in the garage. Darrell was up under the hood of the car next to it.

John said, "Hey."

"Hey. Your—" The mechanic came up from the engine and got a look at John. "What happened to you?"

Turning his gashed temple away: "Nothing."

"Doesn't look like nothing."

"Just banged my head. It was an accident."

"Another accident? You got to be more careful."

For a second John saw himself driving his good fist into Darrell's face. Instead, weary: "I just want to pick up my car."

"She's all yours. I put a new hose in, and she runs like a dream."

"How much?"

"Hundred fifty dollars."

John's jaw went cartoon slack. "How much?"

"Parts, labor; I call it a hundred fifty."

"For a goddamn radiator hose?"

"You know how long it took me to find that hose?"

"About an hour and a half, because that's all the longer I've been gone."

Darrell tilted his head and let a long stream of green-brown something drip from his mouth. He made a face that said: *Look here.* "Now, that's about an hour and a half more than I usually spend looking for parts. You're the one thinks that car's so fancy. What'd you expect but fancy damn prices?"

"That's a Ford, not a Ferrari." Heart pumping like a bad engine. The world started to burn white. "You going to tell me no one else in this shit hole drives a Ford?"

"That's not just a Ford. That's a 'sixty-four-and-a-half Mustang convertible."

John's head cocked from side to side as if trying to shake loose some logic. "What the hell does that have to do with anything?"

"I don't know, but it's the reason I'm living here, and you're just passing through."

A new vision: John's hands at Darrell's throat.

"Look, man; I got rolled half an hour ago for everything I had." He dug in his pocket and pulled out a bill. "Five bucks. That's all I've got on me."

Darrell whipped out a hand and snatched it from him. The mechanic was quick for a slow guy. "Well, then, you're only a hundred forty-five in the hole. Now, why don't you just take your Visa Express silver card, go call Karl Malden, and have him send you the money lickety-split?" He followed that with the crooked, blackened-tooth smile.

"I don't have a credit card. They took my wallet."

"That's too bad. I sure hope you know how to wash dishes, or shovel shit, 'cause you're gonna have to work this one off."

John fumbled at his left wrist, his fingers clumsy with desperation. "How about a watch? Let's say you take my watch and we'll call it even. It's a Movado."

Using the nail of his little finger Darrell dug wax from his ear. The ease of manner with which he performed the chore made it seem more art form than action. "Don't need a watch. 'Sides, I got a thing for cash. I like the way it folds. Now raise on up out of here 'fore you scare off all my business."

"You son-of-a-bitch!"

"Sweet-talk me all you want, but you don't get the keys to that thing till I get my hundred and forty-five dollars."

Darrell went into the station, slamming the door behind him.

John stood alone. In his mind, Harlin's burned to the ground.

———

Hot like an August brushfire. John propped open the phone-booth door with his foot. The air that rushed in was about as cool as a firestorm. He hit "0," then put a finger to the gash on his temple. A disco of lights went off in his head.

An operator came on the line.

"Yeah, I want to make a collect call."

High above Vegas, penthouse suite—a shitty downtown hotel, but penthouse suite—the phone rang. Richie's massive hand swallowed the receiver and lifted it from the cradle.

"Yeah," he grunted.

Across the suite, behind a mahogany desk, in a suit that should have been banned in '79, Mr. Vesci said: "Richie, how many times do I got to tell you? You answer a phone 'hello,' not 'yeah.' You got no manners? What are you? A fucking Neanderthal?"

Richie hung his head: a child caught drawing on the living-room wall. Into the phone he said: "Hello?"

"Mr. Vesci there?"

"Who wants him?"

"It's John Stewart."

Richie curled a hand over the mouthpiece. "It's that deadbeat Stewart. You want to talk to him?"

Mr. Vesci swirled two fingers in the air. Richie brought the phone to him.

Mr. Vesci said: "John, what a surprise. I expected to be seeing you, not talking to you over the phone."

"I know, Mr. Vesci." John's voice was slow and trembled,

as if the words were afraid to leave his mouth. "I know. I was on my way to you. It's just that . . . What a day I've had. You're not going to believe what's happened to me."

Mr. Vesci leaned back in his chair, already bored. "Try me."

"I had the money, I swear I did. I was on my way to you when my car breaks down in the middle of nowhere."

"That's a shame, John." Vesci balanced his checkbook in his head. "A real shame."

"You don't know how. And that's not the half of it. I've got your money, I go into this little grocery store to get something to eat, and it gets robbed."

"And this robber, he gets the money."

"I mean, what are the odds?"

"You're the gambler. You tell me."

Except for an electric hum, the line was quiet.

"I got nothing. I can't even get my car out of the garage. I tell you, Mr. Vesci, if it weren't for bad luck I wouldn't have any at all."

Calmly, quietly: "You're right, John."

"How's that?"

"I don't believe you." Mr. Vesci came forward in his chair. His voice, calm and steady, slid into John's ear like an ice pick. "You listen to me, you deadbeat little fuck: I don't care if your girlfriend chopped off your pecker and fed it to the dog. You owe me money, and I want it. It don't matter to me where from or how. I want it on my desk tomorrow, or I'll show you just how bad your luck is."

Mr. Vesci looked to Richie.

Richie picked up a pen from the desk and snapped it in his hand.

"You understand me, you fuck?"

John mumbled something like a yes.

Mr. Vesci tossed the phone to Richie. He hung it up.

"Fucking kid." Back in the day, Vesci thought, a guy like John'd be dead by now. Those were the times; back when Vegas was still run by guys like Lansky and Costello and Genovese. He recalled them with the same fondness most people remembered a carnival they attended as a child. Those guys understood a debt was a debt, and they knew if you let one go, then every other deadbeat on the Strip would think they could pull something, too. Sure, you come to Vegas for a good time, but no one tells you to bet your retirement money in a backroom card game. It wasn't Vesci's fault. You're not supposed to win. People should know that, and fuck them if they didn't.

But Vegas wasn't run by the boys anymore. Everything was run by corporations in New York, or L.A., that didn't like trouble 'cause everything was family-oriented now, and families weren't supposed to get killed on vacation 'cause it kept the other families away.

Vegas for families? Castles and theme parks and faggots doing magic with white tigers and marks you couldn't out and out kill. What kind of bullshit was that?

Mr. Vesci turned hard on Richie. "And you, breaking the fucking pens. You're a goddamn Neanderthal." He smoothed back his face with his hands and thought for a moment. "Do something useful," he said to Richie. "Find out where that call came from."

Forty minutes in the phone booth: an ant under a magnifying glass on a summer day. Every number he could think of John called. Half wouldn't even accept the charges. Most who did just wanted money he owed them, and weren't trying to hear anything else.

Cici was the last call. His girlfriend. Ex-girlfriend. Most recent ex-girlfriend. Most recent ex-girlfriend before Gayle. A warm, sweet, lovable girl who was good about floating him money.

He made his pitch fast and hard. The big sale, like trying to get Arabs to buy sand. When he got to the part about Mr. Vesci and Richie and the back-alley manicure he got, John started dancing for his life. It was a story of pain, suffering, remorse, and redemption. The way John told it, it was enough to make a skinhead go wet with tears.

When he finished his tale he whimpered slightly, took a long, dramatic pause, and waited for three questions from Cici: Where? When? How much?

She laughed. Not a giggle, or a snort, but a cackle that ran on like the Mississippi. She only stopped laughing long enough to say something about karma, irony, and getting what you deserve. All that was followed by several variations on the word *fuck*.

What was she so pissed about? John thought. She still had his Mr. Coffee machine.

Cici started to tell John she hoped Mr. Vesci would slice him again, and this time not stop until he got down to John's—

John slammed the receiver into the cradle. Again and again and again. "Goddammit! Shit! Damn! Damn! Damn!"

The phone fell from the cradle and twisted slowly by the cord. A voice eeked out. "Hello?"

John grabbed up the phone, a combination of desperation and hope lit his voice. "Hello?"

An operator said, "Please deposit an additional seventy-five cents."

Three times he smashed the receiver into the phone. "Fuck you! Fuck you! Fuck you." Then let it drop.

John kicked open the booth. Glass shattered and fell to the ground like a thousand brilliant snowflakes. He headed off to nowhere.

In the booth, from the phone: "Thank you for using AT&T."

The truck stop was pure roadside kitsch. A linoleum-covered counter trimmed with aluminum. Behind it, in the kitchen, a short-order cook sizzled stuff on an open grill. A waitress—pink uniform, white nurse's shoes, and a bouffant—worked a wad of gum. Two truckers hunched over their coffee. A Wurlitzer parked in the corner rattled off country.

Ed, one of the truckers, said: "Hundred thirteen degrees. That was back in July of 'forty-seven. Ain't no way it's gonna be hotter than that."

Boyd, the other trucker, said: "Hundred and eight already."

John wandered in. The truckers, the waitress, the cook gave him the same "what the hell is that" look most people would give a long-lost piece of food they came across in the back of their refrigerator. John let them have their stares. He fell into a stool at the far end of the counter. His head dropped down into his hands.

The truckers went back to each other.

"Well, hundred eight ain't a hundred and thirteen," Ed said.

"It will be."

"You ain't nothing but an old fool."

"You got two years on me. What does that make you?"

The waitress laid two plates of something greasy in front of them. "Why don't you both shut up and eat?"

"It's Boyd. He's always got to go on about something. The whole ride from Santa Fe he wouldn't shut up about that coin."

"It's true." Some of whatever it was he was eating tumbled from Boyd's mouth.

The waitress asked, "What about a coin?"

"It's nonsense," Ed said.

"It is not," Boyd said.

"A coin's got two sides. You flip it, there's a fifty-fifty chance it'll be heads or tails. Boyd thinks you give a coin ten tosses, it'll come up each side half the time."

"It will."

"No it won't. Not necessarily. You just don't know shit about statistics."

"And what are you? One of them NASER scientists?"

Boyd stuffed a forkful of food in his mouth and bit down. A spray of grease arched across the counter and hit John in the side of the face. His head stayed in his hands.

Ed said: "I got more brains than you've got teeth."

A couple entered. Teenagers. The girl in a dull print dress. The boy buzz cut with cigarettes rolled into the sleeve of his white T-shirt. They slid into a booth.

Boyd said: "Put your money where your chicken-lipped mouth is. I'll bet this morning's pay I'm right."

John's ears went warm. He lifted his head from the counter.

Ed mumbled: "I ain't wasting my money on something so stupid."

The waitress warmed their coffee. "You two are like a couple of children."

All the while John had been doing some figuring. Morning's pay; enough to get the Mustang, to get somewhere, to get some more money and get to Vegas. He looked at his watch. Maybe he could still make it by the end of the day. He said out loud, "I'll take a piece of that bet."

Everyone gave him a second look; long and hard.

Boyd smiled like a weasel come upon a lost chick. "Well, a man with some gumption. How much money you got?"

John remembered Darrell snatching away his last five. "Nothing."

With a laugh: "You want to make a kiddie bet?"

John took off his watch and slid it across the counter. "It's a Movado."

Boyd held it up. "Never heard of it." He looked it over with the same skepticism early man beheld fire. "It's got no day, or date. Shit, it ain't even got any numbers. What's the matter? You couldn't afford a Timex?"

"Next city you're in take it to a jeweler. He won't give you less than two thousand dollars for it."

Boyd chewed at the inside of his mouth, thought. "You're on, mister. You got a coin, Ed?"

He slapped a quarter on the counter. "I want that back when you're finished."

To the waitress Boyd said: "Sugar, you officiate."

"I ain't got time for this."

"It'll only take a minute. Be a gal and help out." He balanced the coin on a bent thumb. "Everybody ready?"

John moved in closer, nodded to Boyd.

"Here we go."

Boyd jerked back his thumb. The quarter twisted into the air, reflecting splinters of sunlight. He caught it, slapped it to the back of his hand.

"One heads," the waitress called out.

The quarter took air again.

"Two heads."

Then three flips; three tails.

The childishness of it all began to wear off. Everyone pressed close, a collective held breath as their heads bobbed up and down with each toss.

Two more flips; both heads.

John felt sweat bead on his neck.

A flip; tails.

A flip; heads.

Boyd held up the quarter. "One more. Tails is five each and I get the watch. Heads, and you is a rich man."

He laid the quarter on the back of his thumb, careful, like coin tossing had become an Olympic event. The flip, the catch, the slap to the back of the hand, and a slow, dramatic reveal.

Heads.

John: "Yes!"

Ed: "Told you."

The waitress: "Stupid. Just plain stupid."

Boyd twisted his lips. He looked down and started to turn away from John.

John shot out a hand and took him firm by the shoulder. "Hey, fair and honest, man." He rubbed his thumb to his fingers. "Pass it over."

Boyd sank a hand into his pocket and pulled out some bills. He tossed them on the counter.

John counted them. Then again. His voice choked. "Thirty dollars?"

"That's my morning's pay."

"I'm a rich man off of thirty dollars?"

With a shrug: "You are around here."

"This is fucking great. I sit there sweating my ass off watching you toss a fucking coin, put a two-thousand-dollar watch on the line for thirty fucking dollars?"

Boyd said quietly, "I thought it was a lot of money." He looked to Ed for support. "Ain't that a lot of money?"

John slumped down into a stool. The waitress came over. She fed herself a few new sticks of gum.

"Now that you're so well-off, can I get you something, hon?"

To the counter John said: "You got beer?"

"What would a truck stop be without beer?"

"Let me have a Beck's."

Her head snapped back like a fighter surprised by a jab. "Beck's? We ain't got any Beck's."

"Kirin?"

"We ain't got any Kirin. We got Miller."

"Genuine draft?"

"No. Miller. Just regalar Miller. You want it, or don't you?"

John let a long, slow, breath slip from his mouth. "Yeah, let me have the Miller."

The short-order cook yelled out from the kitchen. "Flo, order up."

"Be right back with that beer."

John watched her for a while. To himself he said, "A waitress named Flo. Christ."

Something brushed his ankle. He looked down to see a

cat rub up against his leg. It purred softly, licked at his sock, then purred again cute and sweet.

John kicked, and the animal went screeching across the floor. "Fucking cat," he spat after it.

The boy in the booth—buzz cut and cigarettes—got up and went into the bathroom. The girl he was with watched him go, waited a moment, then pushed up from her seat. She went over to the Wurlitzer, looked at it, looked over John. Floating up next to him she smoldered, or came as close as a teenager could.

"Hey, mister. Got a quarter?" She worked her voice, but got more shrill out of it than sexy.

"What?" John didn't even bother with a look in her direction.

"I wanna play a song on the juke. You got a quarter?"

He fumbled a hand in his pocket, found something, and tossed it to her.

"Thanks. Got any requests?" Check out the girl cranking up her "do you want to fuck me" smile. She gave it the best she had, but it glowed with all the seductive intensity of a low-watt bulb.

"That country shit all sounds alike to me."

"How about if I pick something out for you?"

She went to the jukebox and loaded it up. Patsy Cline twanged her way through "Your Cheatin' Heart." The girl took up a stool next to John's.

"You like Patsy Cline? I just love her. How come, I wonder, she don't put out no more new records?"

"She's dead."

The girl's lips went to a pout. "That's sad. Don't that make you sad?"

John, dryly: "I've had time to get over it."

She gave John a curious look. "You're not from around here, are you? Where you from?"

"Oz."

The girl giggled like a tickled baby. "You ain't from Oz. Oz is in that one movie."

"You're too quick for me."

Buzz cut came out of the bathroom. He looked at his girl. He looked at John. He looked at his girl talking to John. With his best imitation swagger he stomped over to them.

"Hey! What are you doing with my girl?"

John gave him all the attention of a buzzing fly.

"I axed you a question."

The girl said: "Aw, Toby, we weren't doin' nothin'. We was just talkin'."

"You shut your mouth, girl, and get back over to our table." Digging up all his manhood, he turned back to John. "Now, I'm not going to axe you again, mister. What were you doing with my girl?"

John finally bothered to look at the boy. Eighteen. Maybe. Dusty jeans, a comb stuck in his back pocket, and what he had for a chest puffed out. He looked like he had read about being tough once in a magazine years ago, but had forgotten all the good parts.

"I wasn't doing anything with your girl."

"That's not the way it looked to me."

"She asked me for a quarter, that's all."

"Looked to me like you were trying to make time with her."

"Make time?" John's eyebrows crashed into each other in the middle of his forehead. "Is everybody in this town slaphappy?"

"Honest, Toby," the girl squeaked. "I just axed him for a quarter for the jukebox."

"I done told you to stay out of this, Jenny. We got man's business to take care of."

"Look, pal, I wasn't making a play for your girl."

"You expect me to believe that?"

"I don't care what you believe as long as you leave me alone."

John started to turn away and get back to doing nothing. Toby took a handful of his shoulder and jerked him back.

"I'm calling you out, mister."

"What?"

"You heard me. I'm calling you out."

"You want to fight?"

"Right here, right now."

"Over her?"

John gave the girl a once-over. Blank paper wasn't as plain.

"You're out of your mind. I'm not fighting over that."

The boy pushed close. "You know who I am, mister? Toby N. Tyler. My friends call me TNT. You know why?"

"They're not very imaginative?"

Toby's breath came hot. " 'Cause I'm just like dynamite. And when I go off, somebody gets hurt."

John sank back on the stool. "Fine. I was making time with your girl. Now I'm all scared, and I'll never do it again. So go away."

"I'll go away. After I settle with you."

"Christ, I don't believe this."

Toby growled, "Stand up."

"I wasn't—"

"Mister, stand up, or I'll beat you where you sit."

John's shoulders fell as he let out a deep breath. There was no getting around it. He stood and put a little distance between himself and Toby. His good hand tightened to a fist.

The girl, lips pulled to a slight smile, bit at a fingernail.

Flo came up between John and Toby. "Wait a second. What's the matter with you two? Wantin' to bash each other's brains in." She looked scornfully from one to the other. "I don't want you bleeding all up in here. Take it outside."

Toby brushed her aside. "Don't you never mind, Flo. This is going to be over real quick."

They stood apart, face-to-face, staring each other down. For a long minute they waited for the other to make the first move. Anyone who knew anything about fighting knew that: Let the other person make the first move. John knew it, and Toby knew it. But Toby got impatient, as children are apt to do. He moved a little, a very little. A dipped shoulder, a slight shift of his weight.

That was plenty for John. He locked an eye on the boy's jaw. His fist, quick back then forward, stiffened for the coming crunch of bone to teeth.

John stopped cold, his fist and cocked arm frozen dead in the air.

The truck-stop door opened. A sheriff walked in. He was pink and sweaty and round. His belt held back his blubbery gut as well as a mud wall would a tidal wave. He sat at the counter, ignoring John and Toby. Two people fighting on a hot day; same as it ever was.

John and Toby stood like bookends. Toby jammed his

hands in his pockets, gave a casual laugh. He stepped to John and hissed in his ear. "You're lucky, mister. Don't think this is over. I called you out and I'm gonna see this through."

To Jenny he said, "Come on, girl. I got half a mind to make you walk home."

Jenny mouthed a silent "bye-bye" to John as Toby pulled her out the door.

From over his shoulder the sheriff watched them go. "What was it about this time?"

The waitress dumped coffee in his cup. "You know how that Toby is. Thinks every man he sees is after his Jenny."

A chuckle rippled across the sheriff's belly. "More like Jenny is after every man she can get."

Flo patted John as she passed. "You don't pay Toby no mind. He just likes to show off for his girl. He's the jealous type. Couple of hours; he'll cool off. You still want that beer?"

John felt the world go tilt-a-whirl on him. He closed his eyes to make it stop, but all he got was a dark tilt-a-whirl. "I'll take it to go."

The truckers took up stools on each side of the sheriff.

Ed asked, "How's it with you, Sheriff?"

"Already starting out bad." He took in some coffee. "Couple of guys tried to knock over Jamilla's grocery store. She got one of 'em. Other one got away."

John turned his shoulder. His right hand covered his blue-black forehead.

"Poor thing," Flo cooed. "She all right?"

"Yeah. Sons-of-bitches tried to steal her wedding ring. That's when she started shooting. Can't blame her. It was all Carlos left her when he died."

John said, "Could I get my beer?"

The waitress shook her head in time to the chewing of her gum, paying as much attention to John as to wind chimes. She said: "Why would someone do something so terrible like try and rob poor Jamilla?"

"It's the heat," Boyd tossed in. "That's what it is. The heat makes everybody crazy. Ain't that right, Sheriff? People go crazy with the heat."

"My beer?"

The sheriff lapped up more coffee. "I seen some bad ones in the heat. Once, a couple of years back on a white-hot day, I had a woman went crazy. Her little baby was so hot it kept cryin' and cryin' all day long. Husband comes home and asks where the baby is. Turns out the wife put it in the freezer to keep it cool."

Everyone was still, like campers gathered round the fire for a ghost story.

John started to say, "Excuse me, could you—"

"Lord," Flo snapped. "Put the baby in the icebox. Killed the poor thing."

The sheriff tossed back the last of his coffee. "Baby didn't die. Just froze off all its fingers and toes. Nothing but a little fingerless, toeless boy now. But the husband, he sees what the wife's done, so after he saves the baby he locks the wife in the refrigerator to see how she likes it. Now, she died. State got around to frying him about a year later. Two people dead, and one boy who won't so much as be able to pick his nose."

Everyone caught a breath: a story well told.

"Flo! My beer!"

The waitress snapped back to real time. "I'm sorry, sugar. I forget about you? You should have said something." She went and fetched.

66

Boyd was still on the sheriff's story. "It's the heat, I tell you. Just gets under a man's skin and turns him crazy."

Ed gave him a backhand to the shoulder. "Come on. That yogurt's got to make Flagstaff while it's still good."

The truckers left. They climbed into their rig, heavy with chrome. It shined under the sun like a disco ball as they drove off.

Flo reappeared at the cash register. "Here's your beer, hon."

John went to her, head turned from the sheriff. He peeled off a five and passed it across the counter.

"Let me change this up." She rang up the sale and started to break the bill.

John eyed the twenty-five dollars in his hand. Hundred twenty more, he could get his car. Thirteen thousand more and Mr. Vesci would let him live.

Maybe.

"Flo, I'm just gonna help myself to a refill." The sheriff hoisted himself from his stool. He stretched across the counter for a fresh pot of coffee.

Like somebody's mother, the waitress said: "Ray, you be careful."

As the words left her mouth the pot fumbled from the sheriff's grip. It flipped in the air, spraying a pinwheel of black lava before smashing against the tile floor.

"Ray!" The waitress ran over to him. "Look what you done. Are you all right?"

The sheriff held his right hand by the wrist. It curled over limp like a dead fish. With the squeal of a stuck pig he said: "I think I burned my gun hand."

"Serves you right." Flo called back into the kitchen: "José, get a mop."

"My gun hand's burned."

John's head raised up. He looked around: Flo nursed the sheriff, the cook was off for a mop, not another soul in the truck stop. The math was easy. His hand slid for the cash register.

Patsy Cline sang "Crazy."

John kept an eye to Flo and the sheriff. He felt the cash drawer, his fingers crept up into it. Paper money crackled under his touch.

A quick, wild screech. Something tore into the back of John's hand. He jerked it up, trailing blood from four deep scratches. By the register drawer arched the cat. It bared its teeth and hissed hard in John's direction.

"Shasta!" The waitress came over. She took up the cat under the forelegs and held it across from her. "Now, why'd you want to scare that nice man like that?"

She set it down on the counter. It looked at John. If the beast could smile, it would have.

"Sorry about that, sugar." The waitress finished making John's change and handed it to him with the beer. "Enjoy that, now." She slammed the register door shut; loud as thunder. "And try and have a nice day."

John went out into the sun.

As he walked on to nowhere John held the beer bottle awkwardly in his bandaged hand and worked the cap with his good one. It held fast. He tightened his grip, turned his shoulder into it. Nothing. He jammed the bottle between his legs, and gripped it with his thighs. Tight hold on the cap, turning from the lower back now. The cap slipped, its edge biting into John's palm.

"Shit!"

A spray of beer came up into him, then fell back into the dirt. Taking the bottle by the neck, John sent it flying end over end, then clutched at his bleeding hand.

"Dammit! Goddammit! I hate this fucking town! Do you hear me? I hate you!" He got done yelling, then got all quiet like the way people do when they slip into shock. To himself he said: "I got to get out of here. I got to get out of this place."

Down the street a storefront, a sign: JAKE McKENNA REAL ESTATE.

It didn't take much thinking before John started toward it.

R ichie hung up the phone. He tore off a piece of paper from a pad and handed it to Mr. Vesci.

"Sierra?" Vesci asked. "Where the hell is that?" He looked over at Richie: a primate who happened to have a decent tailor. "What the hell am I asking you for?"

"What do you want I should do?"

"I want you to get Tony, then I want the two of you to go to this Sierra."

"And . . ."

Mr. Vesci let his head drop back. "I got to draw you a fucking map? Find that Stewart guy, and get my money."

"If he ain't got it you want me to kill him?"

Mr. Vesci closed his eyes and thought of the good old days. The days before Vegas was about water slides and kiddie rides. The days when Vegas was about Vegas, and what Vegas was about was 35 percent off the top, any show-girl you wanted out of the line, and front-row tickets to Frank, or Dean, or Sammy.

Sammy.

There was this one night years ago when they had taken Sammy out into the desert. Not Mr. Vesci personally, but some of the boys had done it. Sammy had been seeing—had been fucking—some Hollywood actress. A nobody, really, but that didn't matter. She was white just the same. No way some monkey was going to fuck a white broad. Not in Vegas. Not in the good old days. So they, the boys, had taken Sammy out into the desert and put a knife to his one good eye and told him he had a day to marry a chick. Didn't matter who, didn't matter what she did, as long as she was a nigger.

Jesus fucking Christ, Mr. Vesci thought. What he wouldn't have given to have been there for that.

And the next day, less than that even, Sammy was married to some low-rent showgirl. Nothing special about her except she was a monkey, too.

Mr. Vesci couldn't help but laugh. True story. Maybe. But it was a good story. There was nothing like a good story to make him feel warm all over.

Richie's voice brought him rushing forty years from the past. "Mr. Vesci, if he ain't got the money, you want me to kill him?"

Fuck this corporate Vegas bullshit. Fuck the theme parks, and roller coasters, and pirate shows, which were about the only place in town anyone ever got killed over money anymore. Every hour, on the hour. Vesci missed the good old days. "Richie, even if he does have it, I want you to kill him."

Richie smiled a pleasant smile. "Thank you, Mr. Vesci."

The secretary was pretty. In most ways worth a second look. John didn't bother with a first. The walk to Jake's office, the reception area, the secretary, they were all just a dull blur. The only thing there was room for in John's head was a dark road that was his sole path to salvation, nothing more.

The secretary ushered him into Jake's office, where the older man sat behind a large, oak desk.

"Thank you, Beth. Why don't you take lunch."

The secretary left, closing the door behind her.

Jake leaned back in his chair, running his eyes up and down John. "Good Lord. What happened to you?"

"Just ran into a little trouble."

Same as if this was the most pitiful thing he had ever seen, Jake shook his head slow. "Another accident? You really must learn to be a wee more careful. Can I get you a drink?"

"No."

"Something to eat?"

"No. I'm okay."

"I thought you'd be halfway to Las Vegas by now."

"I had problems getting my car back."

A knowing smile: "You just seem to attract problems, don't you?"

John let it pass. "Nice office you got."

"I do all right. Real estate isn't a bad game, such as it is round these parts. The land isn't worth much. The trick is to underestimate the price when you buy, and overvalue when you sell. You can turn a few dollars that way."

"Isn't that illegal?"

Jake stared ahead, blank-faced, as if John had said not a word. "Now, what can I do ya for?"

"I was hoping we could talk."

"About?"

"Things. Your wife."

"Sweet Grace? What about her?"

"About what you said this morning."

The older man drew his face tight, as if trying to understand, but having it all just beyond his grasp.

"You said you had an insurance policy out on your wife. Fifty thousand dollars."

"I did?"

"You said you'd cut that up with the man who . . ." Words caught in John's throat. "Took care of things."

"Did I?"

"Don't play simple," John snapped. "You want me to spell it out for you? I'll do Grace if you cut me in on the money."

Jake sat quiet for a long moment. He rocked forward in his chair, resting his elbows on the desktop. "I think the heat's getting to you. You must be touched the way yer rambling."

"I'm not rambling."

"Sure, and yer talking like a madman."

An accusing finger shot out from John's hand. "You're the one who brought it up this morning. In your car."

"That was just loose talk, lad. I don't want to see anyone dead."

"Bullshit! You wanted me to kill her."

"A man doesn't always mean what he says."

"You meant it."

With a laugh: "What makes you say that?"

"Because I think you're a slimy bastard who would have his wife killed just to get his hands on some money."

"And what does that make you?"

"The slimy bastard who's going to kill her for you."

John felt himself wet with sweat. He was getting used to the feeling. Above his head a ceiling fan churned the air, its blades whistled with a dull swoosh.

Jake stood, went to the office door and locked it. He wandered back behind his desk. "Let's say I do want her dead. What is it you want? This morning you weren't a killer."

"This morning I didn't know how badly I'd need to get out of this fucking town."

"And for that you'd kill Grace?"

"For that I'd kill the pope on Easter Sunday."

Jake almost laughed. He said, "Just to get out of here? That doesn't seem much for a murder."

"How do you put a price on killing?"

Shrugging: "I put it at fifty thousand dollars, minus yer cut. Which is?"

Without so much as a casual thought: "Make it twenty."

"Twenty thousand?" Jake sucked air. "I don't have that kind of money. I won't get the insurance till months after she's dead. I don't imagine you'll be wanting to be sticking around after poor Grace's demise. Twenty thousand." Jake made a look of hard thought, then held up his hands in defeat. "That's more money than I could ever get my hands on."

"How much could you get?"

"Maybe . . . maybe ten thousand. And that's a maybe."

"I need thirteen."

"That's a wee much."

"For Christ sake, you're not buying a car. You're having your wife killed. It's thirteen, or it's nothing."

Jake's tongue slid back and forth between his teeth and his lower lip. "You drive a hard bargain, but I had a feeling you were my boy when I met you."

"I'm not your boy, Jake. I don't like you, and I don't like what you are. I've got no choice but to do business with you. This is just a nasty little marriage of convenience."

Jake looked pained. "Don't say that. I had a marriage of convenience with Grace, and look where that got us." He took a breath, long and slow. "Well, looks like we got ourselves a pact."

"Do we shake hands?"

"If you can't trust the man you've hired to kill yer wife . . ."

They stood waist-deep in silence; high-schoolers at the end of a first date waiting for the other to make the first move.

John: "I guess I might as well get this done with."

"The sooner it's over with, the sooner yer on yer way. Now listen to me." Jake's voice went soft. It drew John in. "It's got to look like an accident, that's the thing. If it doesn't, then it's no good. I won't get a dime, and it's my neck that'll be on the chopping block while yer living it up somewhere."

"What should I do?"

"How should I know, for·frig sake? I never had a wife killed before. I guess I should have hired a professional."

"You want to do this yourself?" Wild gestures came from John's arms.

"Quiet, lad. I'm thinking." Jake sank into his chair. Fingers knitted, he bit at the flesh. "It can't be done at the house. It should be . . ." He laid his palms flat on the desktop. "This is what you do: Go to the house to see her—"

"And tell her what?"

"I don't know. Tell her you had to see her. Tell her you don't care if she's married or not, you just had to be with her. A buck like yerself must be good at shellacking a line, or two."

John slid his teeth against each other, but said nothing.

"Then ... maybe shift the conversation. Get her talking about that Jeep of hers. She loves that thing." He tossed in a spiteful laugh and added, "Maybe the only thing she does love. She'll want to take you for a ride."

Jake looked out the window behind him over the endless miles of sun-licked dirt. "She'll take you out there somewhere. Always was fond of the red rock and mesas. So am I." He slowed. "I guess we have that in common." Back into it. "She'll ride you out someplace quiet, deserted. No one for miles. Just the two of you, and some prairie dogs. Sweet-talk her a little, if you like. Makes me no never mind. Just put her at ease, make her feel relaxed, then ..."

Voice cold and steady, John said: "Then do it."

High noon, hottest day of the year. Feel the cold.

Jake stared down at his desktop as if some sacred piece of knowledge had been carved there. As if, maybe, the meaning of life was hidden in the grain of the dark wood. And if he could just look at it long enough, and hard enough, every dilemma would become clear; every problem would be resolved. There was nothing there for him. The answers to his problems lay elsewhere. Jake looked up.

John was gone.

Problem solved.

race leaned up against the wall just inside the screen door. It was the only thing separating her from John. Nothing but fine wire mesh stood in the way of him, and him getting out of Sierra. Nothing but a screen door. For the moment it might as well have been a minefield edged with barbed wire.

The door threw a shadow across Grace. Her sweet voice came out of the dark from a faceless body. "Well, well. Look who it is. Come to get even with me?"

"I came to get something."

The faceless body moved. Maybe there was a smile. "You look like shit."

"Don't hold back, Grace. What do you really think?"

"What happened?"

"Few too many chances. And if you're even thinking about telling me to be more careful, don't."

"Think you'll make it through the day?"

He shrugged. "Your husband let me live."

"Oh yeah," Grace said, same as if recalling a minor plot point of some movie she'd seen years ago. "I suppose I owe you an apology."

"Why'd you do it, Grace?"

Her bare foot scratched at her calf. Man, what a calf. "Why'd the jackrabbit jump out into the middle of the road?"

John nodded. "I'm kind of hot out here."

"You look cool enough under the porch."

"Not that kind of hot."

Grace stepped from the shadows to the light and pressed up against the screen door. It flattened her breasts, and pushed them up from under the fabric of her dress. She got all Southern belle: "Mr. Stewart, I'm a married woman."

Straight-faced, quick and cool: "Do I look like I care?"

Lips pulled back in a wry smile, Grace made a show of thinking things out. "I guess I could let you in, fix you up a little."

"If I promise to be a good boy?"

"If you're gonna be a good boy, you can leave right now."

John sat on the edge of the bed. Grace hitched up her dress and straddled him. She dabbed a cotton ball with alcohol, then pulled his head to her chest.

"No peeking." She giggled.

John got a noseful of her. She smelled fresh and good. She smelled like a woman.

Grace said: "This might hurt a little."

She pressed the cotton ball to the gash on John's forehead. He jerked away from her.

"Ahh! Damn."

"You got to be cruel to be kind. Getting some stitches wouldn't be a bad idea."

"Neither would a trip to Hawai'i, but I'm not getting that either."

"I don't suppose you'd tell me what happened?"

"A couple of guys in leather beat me up over my book bag, so the old Spanish lady tore one of them to shreds."

Grace considered this. "Sounds about right."

She bandaged John's head and the scratches on his hand. She did it sweet, and slow, and full of love. "All done."

"Don't give up so quick. Look hard and who knows what you'll find."

Grace smiled, but got up.

"Weeeell . . ." John pressed himself up from the bed. "I guess that's it."

Back turned to him, Grace asked: "You never did tell me what it is you want."

He started to say something, then pulled it back.

"John," she whispered. "What do you want?"

"I want to hit the numbers. Twenty-two, or thirteen, or zero, or wherever I lay my money. I want to pitch the dice and see them roll natural."

"Jesus, are you talking about gambling again? Are you addicted, or something?"

"Yeah. I guess. Drugs, booze; it doesn't matter. There's no high like seeing the ball drop into the slot you've bet, or looking under your cards and having a jack and an ace look back."

"But you can't win at it. That's why it's called gambling. If you could win it'd be called winning."

"And if you could win all the time it wouldn't be a rush. I'd take a hundred losses, a thousand, just to know what it feels like to hit the big win once."

With her hand Grace ran back her hair. "Except you don't lose for nothing. It costs. I took a gamble with Jake, and I'm still paying for it. Don't take me wrong, John, but I don't know you're the kind of person who can pay the price for losing."

John went to the window. He looked out across the desert; sand, dirt, cactus, tumbleweed. Only the strong survived the desert. The rest was dead. And nothing affected the dead. Not the sun, or rain, or wind. Nothing. When everything else there ever was was gone, if the entire Earth burned to cinder, there would still be desert. The desert was perfect. The desert was forever.

He said: "Nice Jeep you got."

They drove. Twenty minutes, half an hour, straight on into the scorched land. Grace let the Jeep run like a wild horse, and rode it just as hard. She went out of her way to find dunes and gullies, and hit them at full throttle. A brief flight, a spray of dirt, before the Jeep slammed back to the ground.

She laughed like a schoolgirl.

John gripped hard on the roll bar, his hand drained white.

Grace took the Jeep to the high ground, finally letting it rest on a plateau above the desert floor. John slid out to the ground, sat beneath the Jeep's shadow. Grace walked in the sun.

Hand to his brow, he looked out after her. "Doesn't this heat bother you?"

"Yeah, but I like the sun. I grew up on a reservation. The sun, the desert; they were like a religion to us. Jake's the same; he loves the desert. I guess we're alike that way."

"You love him?"

"No."

"Did you ever?"

"Depends on what you call love. When I was growing up I had nothing. I learned to want everything. I wanted more than Sierra anyway, and I would have done anything to get it. Jake was my ticket.

"He's not much, but he's got more money than half this town put together. He was older than me, different from me, but I wanted him. I wanted what he could give me, anyway. So, I courted him. I let him think he was courting me, but I reeled him in like a fish on a line.

"Is that love?"

John didn't bother giving it much thought. "I'm guessing no."

"Yeah, I guess not."

"And I take it things didn't much work out the way you planned."

"I'm still here, aren't I? See this?" Grace swept her hand before her in a wide arc. "All this nothing? I've spent my life in this stinking desert. It doesn't get to Jake the way it gets to me. He doesn't mind being out here. It doesn't bother him to be nothing but a land broker. 'Big fish in a small pond,' he says. More like a little fish in a dried-up watering hole."

"You could leave him."

"I don't know how."

As if nothing were more obvious: "You just walk away."

"It's not that easy. Maybe you can take chances; wander around like some stray wherever you please. I can't. I don't want to be alone. I need to know I'm going to be taken care of."

"You need a meal ticket is what you mean." John talked like he had salt in his mouth. "You need some guy you can latch onto just long enough to get out of here."

"Is that so bad? It's not like I wouldn't try to make him happy. For a while anyway. I mean . . ." Grace tried to sound subtle, but it just made her sound sexy. "I would do things for him. I guess I'm no good that way. I guess I tried to sucker you along like that."

She turned sharply back to John and stared at him across the stretch of dirt that stood between them. "Do you hate me for it? I wouldn't blame you if you did. But maybe it's like you said: You just got to pick up and do whatever it takes to get out."

John whispered softly after her. "Whatever it takes."

Grace stepped to the edge of the plateau. She wrapped herself in her arms and gazed out into the ocean of sky. "You know what I wish?" she asked of no one in particular. "I wish I was a bird. I know it's stupid. Every child says that. When I was growing up some of the old ones on the reservation believed people really could change into animals." Grace spread her arms, ready to take flight. "I wish I could."

John looked over at her, at her back to him. Her feet at the edge of the plateau. He stood and crept for Grace.

Awander in her mind, Grace went on, oblivious to John. "If I was a bird I would fly to Florida, to Disney World. I always wanted to go there. I'd fly to New York. Maybe. I guess New York isn't a very good place to be a bird."

Creep, creep, creep.

"I'd fly to St. Louis—I want to see that arch—to New Orleans, I'd fly all over Texas. Then I'd fly to California. San Diego, and Santa Barbara, and Los Angeles. People say Los Angeles is shit now with the crime and the traffic. I don't care. I want to see Venice Beach, and I want to see Beverly Hills and Bel-Air and Malibu. I want to see all those big fancy houses. I . . . I just . . ." She faltered. "I just want to live."

John crept closer. Right up behind her. Quiet baby

steps, breath held. No sound, except his heart banging away in his chest. He was sure the thunder of it would make her turn around.

Grace kicked a stone from the plateau. She watched it tumble through the air and shatter against the rocks far, far below.

"They say you don't feel a thing," she whispered. "The shock is supposed to kill you before you hit the ground. I don't know how anyone would know that, but I heard it's just like flying. Flying straight down into the ground. I guess if it doesn't hurt, it's a beautiful thing."

Fingers spread, John let them hover behind Grace's back. His heart jumped and thudded like it was trying to pound its way out of him. John rocked back ready to throw his weight forward.

Grace turned suddenly. There was John, inches from her, moving forward. Startled, she went back; feet slipping, arms whipping through empty air for something to grab hold of. She started backward over the ridge.

Hands on her waist, John snatched her forward. Grace's right foot kicked at the ridge, trying to find purchase. It took hold. She dangled there, on the edge of the plateau, sixty or more meters above the ground. Her weight, her life, full in John's hands.

She made no effort to grab hold of him. Grace let her arms dangle free at her side, and got all relaxed, arched her back some into John's hands the way you do when you're trying to scratch an itch. It freaked John a little. There she was, hanging between life and death, and she decides to get sexy.

A casual look down at the earth below, then up into his eyes. "Hate's a funny thing," she said, sexy in voice, too.

"Right now I bet you don't know if you want to kill me, or fuck me."

John stared at Grace in his hands. To let her go would take nothing. Literally nothing. Relax his grip, open his fingers, and she would be gone.

He stared at her. What was she to him? A woman who would let her husband beat him bloody. A woman he didn't even know existed six hours ago. Relax his grip, open his fingers, and what did she become? Smashed bones, torn flesh. Thirteen thousand dollars. Freedom.

He stared at her.

He pulled her close, and kissed her hard on the lips.

Noon was the hottest part of the day. John had always figured that, at least. Maybe that's the way it worked in the rest of the world. But in this place, this thing that passed for a town but was more like the canvas of a nightmare, noon was just foreplay. The heat was only getting started in Sierra.

He sat on the edge of the bed, shirtless, sweaty, looking out the window. Somewhere, miles out into the desert, he had traded his freedom in for a good fuck.

A great fuck.

John and Grace had had that kind of sex which starts in the hall on the way to the bedroom 'cause you're too horny to wait for something soft to screw on. The sex went down a wall, to the floor—tumbling around more than a few times while clothes were awkwardly sheared off—over up against some furniture as bodies tussled probing, looking, feeling for matching parts. Then the sex went one more time toward the bed, because that's where—instinctively—it figured it should be. It never actually made it. Things got finished up next to the dust bunnies in the corner.

In fact, in the end, the only thing the bed was good for was resting after the workout was well over.

Grace lay next to John, naked, sweaty, stroking his

back. The sun tore through the window and glistened off the sheen on their bodies.

"How far is it to California?" she asked.

"From here? I don't know. Far. Far enough."

"Have you been there before?"

"Yeah."

"Is it pretty?"

John nodded. "Beautiful. Beautiful beaches. Blue water and blue skies as far as you can see."

Grace sat up. She slid her hands under John's arms to his chest and pulled him close. Her erect nipples poked at his back.

She said, "Take me with you."

To the point: "I can't."

"Please. I won't hang on you. As soon as we get there, you can dump me. I don't care. I just want to get out of here."

"Grace, I can't. I can't even get out of here myself. I need a hundred fifty bucks just to get my car from that crazy mechanic."

Lips pressed to John's cheek, Grace's breath came hot in his ear. "I know where we could get money. A lot more than one hundred fifty dollars."

John rounded the edge off his curiosity. "Where?"

"Jake." She stroked at his back again.

"You think Jake's going to give me money just so I can take you out of here?"

"He doesn't give it to us." Her fingernails ran the length of his spine. Five red lines raised up on his back. "We take it," she said.

"Take it? Take it from where?"

"Jake's got money. In a floor safe in the living room. He talks about it all the time. More like brags. He loves his money. Wouldn't think of spending a little on me."

"You live all right."

"Yeah. A bird in a gilded cage."

John worked hard to sound casual. As casual as someone could when talking about someone else's money. "How much has he got?"

"Near as I can figure, must be about . . . one hundred thousand dollars."

"One hundred . . ." Before he could stop himself: "That son-of-a-bitch lied to me."

"Lied? What do you mean?"

"I . . . nothing. Just something he said." Moving on quick: "So, if the money's in a safe, you'd have to get the combination—"

"No. It takes a key. Jake wears it on a chain 'round his neck. He keeps it on him all the time. I mean all the time. It scratches up against me when we do it." Grace got up and slipped into her sundress. Most women looked better clothed than naked. Some were built well enough to look good in the raw. Grace was the rare kind of woman who looked good any way she came.

"If the key's on him, to get it we'd have to . . ."

Fluffing her hair: "We'd have to kill him." It came out that simple.

At first nothing. Then, from deep inside, a laugh erupted from John, long and hearty. It kept coming like waves on a beach. "I think this heat is making me crazy." He jammed his arms down the sleeves of his shirt and buttoned it as fast as his bad hand would let him. "I was crazy to come back here. I'm crazy for listening to anyone in this town, and I'd sure as hell be crazy if I spent another minute in this place."

"John, please—"

"I don't know what I was thinking, but I can't do it."

"What are you talking about?"

"Kill someone. I can't do it."

Like the only thing he was fretting about was the weather, Grace said: "Is that all?"

"Is that all? Jesus Christ, you're talking about murder." John pressed himself up against a dresser. His breath came in short fast huffs.

"Is it so bad? It would be quick. He wouldn't even have to feel it." As Grace talked she floated up behind John. "Sometime in the middle of the night. When it's quiet, when he's asleep. You just come up on him slowly, softly, and . . ."

She lay her hands on John's back. It came as a surprise, like the quick slash of a knife. He jumped hard.

"Shit!"

"It's not like he's a young man. He's had time to live."

John's lips fluttered, trying to grab hold of the right words. "Jesus, listen to yourself! You're all insane. Every one of you. Not me, Grace. Mark me absent. I don't want any part of it." He went for the door.

"John!" Grace took John hard by the arm. The strength of her grip surprised him. "Listen to me! I grew up on a reservation. A fucking patch of desert in the middle of nowhere. That's where they stick the Indians. That's where they leave us to die.

"My mother died there. My father died there. I had a brother who killed himself at twenty-two because he couldn't take it anymore."

John tried to pull away. Grace dug her fingers to his bone.

"There's no hope there, John. I was lucky to make it this far. You've got to do this for me. I'll do anything for you." She took his eyes deep into her own. "Anything."

For a moment John felt himself drowning in her. He felt as if there was no point in fighting, and for a moment he didn't want to. There was a bliss and a nirvana that came just beyond letting go. He knew it was the rapture. He knew it was the feeling that came when death was present, and the only thing left was to give in. But a thought came to him: Whose death was it?

Yanking himself free of Grace, John bolted for the door like a diver breaking for the surface.

Grace gave chase. "How are you going to get out of here? You need money. It's not much for a hundred thousand dollars."

John was out the screen door, slamming it shut behind him. Grace yelled after.

"Whatever it takes, remember?"

John headed down the road at a dead run. A cloud of dust kicked up from his feet.

Grace, to herself: "Whatever it takes."

"It's the heat that makes you crazy." It's the old blind man talking. "I don't know what it is, but it works that way for man and animal alike. I seen some peculiar things on a too-hot day. I seen a scorpion sting itself to death. It just keeps drivin' its tail into its body again and again. A little killer killing itself.

"Seen a coyote kill itself, too. Just kept on biting and tearing at its own legs. Near tore one clean off before it bled to death.

"And what a man'll do on a hot day . . . A man could get hisself killed just for rubbing shoulders with another.

"I don't know what it is about the heat. I figure it's sort of like putting a kettle of water over a fire. People is mostly water. We boil when it's hot. 'Cept when we boil, the water's got nowheres to go. It just churns inside of us until we can cool off. If it's not too late."

John took up a spot on the curb next to the old man. He swatted flies from the dead dog. "You sure seen a lot for a blind man."

"Just 'cause you ain't got eyes doesn't mean you can't see."

"That a fact?"

"I can see you just fine, for example. You're a young man who thinks he's got someplace to be."

John looked the old man in the sunglasses. It was the closest he could come to making eye contact. "Maybe I do."

"Or maybe you just think you do. You can run just as fast and far as you like, but wherever you go, there you are."

Unimpressed: "I think I've heard that one before."

"What do you 'spect for free?"

"You sure got a lot of philosophy, old man."

"That's 'cause I've done a lot of living."

"Maybe one day I can sit on a corner and spout wise."

"Think you'll live that long?"

The old man's words hit like a blackjack. John staggered up to his feet. The old man rattled some coins in a dented, dusty tin cup.

"Ain't you got a little something for the infirm?"

"I'm kind of short right now. I'll catch you next time." John walked away.

The old man's head lolled from side to side as if he were trying to locate John with his nose. "I won't hold my breath."

John wandered around aimlessly. Ever since he hit town he was getting good at it. The problem with wandering aimlessly in a place like Sierra is that it doesn't get you very far. He passed the same places over and over again. The same post office/bus stop, the same truck stop. And the spot where he first caught a look at Grace. One day, he thought, someone ought to put a plaque there: THIS IS WHERE HELL BEGINS. From the moment he laid eyes on her, trouble had only been thirty seconds behind. At best she was no good. At worst she was evil. The bitch of it was, like most women who were somewhere between no good and evil, she was the best fuck he ever had.

Eventually John got around to going back to Jake's office. The secretary was gone. Jake was there. He was still seated behind his desk going about business as if nothing unusual were happening that afternoon. Least of all that he was having his wife murdered. He looked up when John entered.

You ready for how cool he is? "How did it go?" That's all he's got to say. Not an anxious bone in his body. Jake might as well have been asking John how was breakfast.

"I went to your place," John started. "We talked. We drove out to the desert . . ."

"But is the job done?" Finally a little deliberation crept into his voice.

"No."

A beat.

"No, you didn't kill her?"

"The time wasn't right."

Jake jabbed an envelope with a letter opener and tore a gash across the top. He gave a quick scan to the enclosed letter before tossing it aside.

He said: "Yer alone, out in the desert, in the middle of nowhere with no one for miles around, and you say the time wasn't right? What's the matter? Maybe you wanted a few more witnesses? Maybe you were hoping to get it on video? A keepsake for the grandkids. 'Look, children, here's where yer grandpapa let a woman have it. Thank God I waited, or I never would've had it on tape.' "

John was at a loss. He wasn't sure how to respond to being reprimanded for screwing up a murder. He settled for: "You know what I mean."

"Ahhh." Jake flipped a hand in John's direction. "I know all right. I know yer just enough a piece of shit to have a go at bedding a man's wife. Sure and you've probably bagged a few at that.

"You'd probably lie, cheat, and steal without thinking twice about it. From that you'd just turn and walk away.

"But to kill; to get the blood on yer hands . . . ? Not so much just to wash that off. You'd be marked for life, just like Cain. And yer a sinner wants to walk with the saints. Ain't that right, lad?"

"You know so much about killing, why don't you do it yourself?"

Jake's shoulders lifted and fell. "I guess I've what you call a love-hate relationship with Grace."

"You love her, but you hate her?"

"No. I hate loving her. I hate the kind of person she is. I hate having to tolerate the little games she plays. I hate letting her use me. But I love her too much to do otherwise, and I for sure love her too much to kill her.

"I couldn't stand to watch her eyes roll back in her head as she sucks her last breath. If I had to see her pretty pink brains spill out of her skull, I think I'd near choke on my own vomit.

"But you? You've got the killing in you."

A little laugh from John, as if Jake had just come to the punch line of a long and amusing story. "You don't know what you're talking about."

"Come close this time, lad, and it scares ya."

Jake's voice screeched in John's ears; steel wheels. He felt himself flush. "Leave it, Jake."

"And next time? Next time somebody's going to get hurt bad."

"Shut up!"

"Next time somebody's going to get dead."

"SHUT UP!"

The wheels came louder, and John climbed back up on that tilt-a-whirl. Next thing he knew, his curled hands were going for Jake's neck.

With surprising speed, and ease, Jake took the younger man by the shoulder. Twisting him, Jake stretched John across the top of the desk, sending up a wave of loose papers.

John tried to scramble to his feet. A sharp pain at his throat. The tip of the letter opener broke his flesh.

Jake sneered down at the boy. "Like I said; next time someone gets dead. Best make sure it ain't you."

After a tense moment Jake eased his grip. John stood, collected himself, trying his best to look as if nothing more had happened than a trip over a curled rug. He wiped away the trickle of blood that dripped from his throat. Just one more wound to add to the collection.

"There's not going to be a next time." John was all calm and controlled. "Nobody's going to get dead. Not by me. Sorry we couldn't do business, Jake. I'm getting kind of attached to this place. Maybe one day you could sell me a retirement plot."

John went for the door. He stopped and turned back. "Jake, how much were you going to pay me to do the job?"

"Thirteen thousand dollars. Had ya done it." He put a little on that last part. "Isn't that what we agreed on?"

"Yes. Yes it was. You think that's a lot of money?"

"All I have in the world."

All smiles. "That's what I like about you, Jake. For a son-of-a-bitch you're an honest man."

omewhere along the way John figured he was heading back to Harlin's. Two reasons: It'd been a while since he'd been there, and he had nowhere else to go. Maybe he could get Darrell to come around. Maybe he could work a deal. Maybe somewhere along the walk to the gas station, Elvis might drop from the sky with thirteen thousand dollars. Plus one fifty for the Mustang. Freshly minted. In a Louis Vuitton suitcase. A voice snapped him back to reality.

"Mister!" Jenny chased down the street after John, her arms churning up air. "Hey, mister. I just . . ." She caught up to him. Short of breath, she bent at the waist and sucked air. Coming up, she said: "I just wanted to thank you."

"For what?"

"For defending my honor this afternoon."

"Hate to burst your bubble, but I wasn't defending you."

Jenny's hands snaked up John's arm. "But you were going to fight for me."

"I wasn't going to fight for you. I was just going to beat the shit out of that punk boyfriend of yours."

Jenny tried to look indignant by way of pouted lips. "He's not my boyfriend. I mean, I let him take me out and stuff, but I ain't spoken for. Not yet, that is."

John shook free of the snakes. "Get this through your head, little girl. I'm not going for you. If this Toby guy likes you, then if I were you, I'd marry him. You're not going to get much better in this town."

"That's what I thought. Until you came ridin' in." She pressed her less than full chest up against him. "I saw your car over to Harlin's. It's cool. Want to go for a ride? Desert's kind of lonely this time of day."

Taking her by the shoulders, John pushed the girl back to arm's length. "How old are you?"

"Eighteen. Well, I will be in two and a half years. But that don't mean you can't take me for a ride if you want."

"No, I do not want to take you for a ride. What I want is for . . ." John thought. "You don't happen to have a hundred fifty dollars I could—"

A voice cracked like weak thunder. "Mister!"

John's eyelids slid down. "Oh shit."

"That's right, mister. You better be afraid." Toby came strolling up the street, growling like a pit bull in a kindergarten. "I told you it wasn't over, but you didn't listen. Now I find you sneakin' around makin' time with my girl behind my back."

"I wasn't making time with . . ." Jenny's shoulders still in his hands, John realized the uselessness of this route. He said to her, "Tell him we weren't doing anything."

Jenny turned to the boy, her head stuck forward, sassy, as far as her neck would allow. "You're too late, Toby. We're going to get in this man's fancy car and ride off and leave you behind."

Check out John's jaw hanging limp, just flapping in the breeze. *"What the hell are you talking about?"*

Pulling her neck in and turning back to John, Jenny asked, "What's your name, anyway?"

That was like pouring gas on a fire. "Oh, that's it." Toby's pale skin went red. "That tears it, mister. I'm gonna bust you up but good. I'm gonna bust you into a million pieces and then . . ." He thought about it. "Bust those pieces up, and then . . ." Toby gave this one a good working over.

John figured at any second the boy would start bleeding from the ears.

"And then I'm going to spread the pieces all around. That's what I'm gonna do. You don't know who you're dealin' with, mister. I'm crazy. I'm psycho crazy."

"Yeah, I know. You're TNT; just like dynamite. When you go off somebody gets killed." John's head twisted from side to side in frustration. At this point he figured it would be just as easy to knock the kid senseless as it would be to talk him down. "All right. Let's do it."

Jenny pushed up between them. "Toby Tyler, it don't matter to me if you beat him all up, and knock out all his teeth, and he's drooling and bleeding all over hisself. We love each other and we gonna run off, and I'm gonna have his love child."

"Will you shut up!"

Toby pushed the girl out of the way. "You're gonna pay for that, mister."

John's fingers snapped into a fist. This time no waiting. He knew how he would play it: a punch to the nose hard and fast. Broken bone, blood; that would break the boy's spirit.

Toby moved forward.

Good, John thought, let him walk into it. Let's get this shit over with. His hand jerked back and hurled forward.

A voice caught it in mid-flight.

"Toby!"

Toby turned. "Sheriff Potter."

The sheriff leaned up against his patrol car. Dig him, looking like he was watching a parade go by. "Toby, I just come from your mother's place. She's worried sick about you. Says she ain't seen you since this morning."

"That ain't true, Sheriff. I was home for lunch."

The sheriff held up his hand. "I ain't trying to hear that right now, boy. Run on home."

Toby looked down at the ground, mashed a heel into the dirt. "Yes, sir." He took Jenny by the wrist. "Come on."

"I wanna stay."

"I said, come on!"

Jenny reached an arm out to her dream man, her hand twisted at him in the air. "Bye, mister. Don't go nowhere without me. I wanna have your love child. I wanna love you."

Toby jabbed a finger toward John. "Next time, mister. Next time."

John walked to the sheriff, who shook his head after Toby. "Kids."

"That boy's a real hothead."

The sheriff gave a laugh. "He is at that. Not much fault of his own. Had quite a trauma as a child."

"What happened?"

"His old man worked in a strip mine north of here. The school takes field trips up to there every year. Big day for the kids when they get to see ore tore up out of the land. Anyhow, one year Toby's class went up there, and on this particular day Toby's father up and falls into the machinery."

"Jesus."

Nodding: "Yep. Tore him up, and spat out little refined pieces of him. Nothing like the embarrassment of having your father refined in front of your classmates to put the anger in a young man."

"I guess."

"Like I said; you really can't blame the boy. Some people don't know how to avoid trouble. Know what I mean?"

Sheriff Potter tossed out the words the way a fisherman casts a line.

John didn't bite.

The sheriff lifted his hat, the brim round and wide like the kind Canadian Mounties wore. The hat left a red line across the middle of his forehead. He snapped out a handkerchief, formerly white, now a dull yellow, and worked it over his sweaty face. He looked up at the sun with squinted eyes. "No mercy for the suffering." The hat went back on. "I saw you at the truck stop this morning. Not from around here, are you?"

"No, sir. And I'm not going to be around long if that's what you're worried about."

"Just curious." Using his jaw to point: "That's a nasty cut you got."

John put a finger to the gash above his eye. Pain came like a field-goal kicker had just put his head through the uprights. "Not as bad as it looks."

"There was a young man over at Jamilla's today when it got robbed. Way she tells it, he got whacked around by one of the robbers."

Poker-faced: "Wouldn't know anything about it."

"That's too bad. I was hoping it might have been you. Maybe you could help us catch the guy who got away. Or maybe you could explain about all that money that got tore up when Jamilla shot that biker."

John turned down the corners of his mouth. "Wish I could help, Sheriff." He spoke as if truly frustrated by his impotence. "If you'll excuse me, I'm going over to Harlin's, picking up my car and getting the hell out of here."

"Stay as long as you like, son. No rush."

"Maybe not for you, Sheriff"—giving a look around at the miles of nothing that was Sierra—"but I think I've had enough of your little town."

The day crawled on.

On a street corner a dog licked at the drip from a fire hydrant. The water was warm, but it was water.

An old woman sat in her house, shades drawn, in a dark corner next to a refrigerator, fanning herself. She wanted to sleep, but was afraid. Her husband lay down to sleep on a hot day once. He never woke.

Behind his house Toby boxed his shadow, his brain hopped up on rage.

Two men in a silver Lincoln Town Car turned off the highway onto a road that would take them the rest of the way from Las Vegas to Sierra.

John came up on Darrell, in Harlin's garage, cleaning his tools. The Mustang, washed, sat gleaming under the dull light.

Darrell said, "Hey. I was beginning to think you wasn't comin' back. You don't look so good."

John stroked a hand across the hood of the Mustang the

way most men would pet a long-lost lover. "Yeah, well, I've been around the bend some today."

"One of those days you feel like you been runnin' and runnin', but you ain't no closer to where you tryin' to get than when you started."

"You been there?"

The mechanic's head bobbed. "I've had days I would gladly trade with a whippin' dog. Ain't much you can do when you feel like that 'cept tough it out."

"You believe that?"

"Think bad, and bad is what you get."

John considered this. "That's a good piece of advice."

Darrell's crooked, blackened-tooth smile: "No charge."

"Listen, Darrell, about the hundred fifty bucks for the car, I swear as soon as I get where I'm going—"

"Two hundred."

"What?"

"The car. It's gonna cost you two hundred dollars."

John's head cocked sideways, then came back around to the mechanic. "You said this morning the hose was one fifty."

"Yep. For the hose. While you was gone I replaced a gasket. That's going to cost you another fifty."

"I didn't tell you to replace any gasket."

"The one you got was shot."

"I didn't tell you to replace any fucking gasket!" Spittle flew with the words. "You can't do unauthorized work!"

"Unauthor . . ." Darrell chewed the word around. "Now you gonna roll out the big words, huh? I guess you know all there is about being a mechanic. I can't do unauthored work?" He let himself have a good laugh. "I suppose what I can do is let you drive out of here on a bad gasket. Then you get in an accident and get killed. Or worse. Who they gonna blame then? They gonna blame me, and there goes my reputation."

"What reputation? You're nothing but an ignorant, inbred, tumbleweed hick."

Darrell narrowed his eyes. It was like a neon sign that said: I'M THINKING. "Is that an insult? Are you insulting me?"

John pushed up close. "Listen, you stupid fuck! I want my car!"

"Take it. As soon as I get my money. Fifty dollars for an almost new gasket. You don't know what kind of deal you're getting."

Slow, deliberate: "I'm taking my car, and I'm taking it now."

"This car ain't going nowheres until I get paid. And if it takes you another five hours, I'll find another fifty dollars of work to do on her. Now raise on up out of here." Darrell rubbed a greasy finger under his nose. "You're stinking up my garage."

John turned to walk away. The world was crazy, wild, and hot; the ground slid under his feet. He reached for a workbench to steady himself, hand brushing up against a wrench.

No time, no thought. Everything happening at once: a grab, the wrench cold and heavy to the touch. A turn, quick. His arm came around fast, high, ready to strike down hard. Ready to crush. Ready to kill.

John stopped dead.

Darrell held a crowbar in a batter's stance, set to send it into the Mustang.

"You want to play, mister? I'll play with you. You want to smash something? So do I."

The mechanic twisted back for the home-run swing.

"No!" The word exploded out of John.

"What's the matter? The fight gone out of you? I'm just gonna smash a headlight. Maybe two."

"Darrell, don't do it!"

"What's the big deal? It's only a 'sixty-four-and-a-half Mustang convertible."

"Look." John stooped. "I'm putting the wrench down." He laid it on the floor. It clanked against the cement.

Giddy with himself: "What, you don't want to play no more?"

"Please, just leave the car alone."

"Yeah, you better remember that."

Darrell lay the tip of the crowbar on the Mustang's hood. John's heart skipped.

"Now get out of here. And you better come up with my money." Pulling back his hand, the crowbar bit into the sheetmetal, leaving a curl of torn paint.

John screamed the way a man does when forced to watch his woman brutalized: weak and impotent. "Goddamn you! You son-of-a-bitch!"

"There you go sweet-talking me again."

A laugh rolled from Darrell, thick and heavy. It swept over John and carried out into the desert.

Stumbling the streets of Sierra. Again. No place for John to go, nothing to do. Again. There was little left for him but to bake in the sun.

Someone spoke.

Stopping, turning. "What?" John asked.

There was no one behind him. He looked around, but the streets were barren. The humanity of Sierra had taken refuge in cool, dark places.

John walked on. No sooner than he had started, the voice spoke to him again. Jake. Far away, but so clear.

"You've got the killing in you," Jake said. He waited, then said it again.

Finger to his ear, John tried to plug the voice out. It only made it louder.

Jake said, Jake screamed: "Maybe not this time, but somebody's going to get dead around you."

John clamped his hands over his ears. He kept them locked there until another voice filled his head. It was his own wailing: "No!"

John's eyes sprang open same as a sleeper startled awake by a nightmare. The first thing he saw was the sign: UNITED STATES POST OFFICE. Below that: GREYHOUND. He felt like a busted gambler who finds a dollar on a casino floor: fresh with possibilities.

The Town Car, dusted over from the back roads, rolled into Harlin's. Richie heaved himself from inside, and was slapped in the face by the heat.

"Jesus fucking Christ. It's hotter than fucking hell out here."

Inside the car Tony bobbed his head while he chewed gum. He didn't make it look easy.

Richie looked around for signs of life. "Hey, Tony, hit the horn."

Tony pressed his fat hand to the center of the steering wheel. Somewhere in the distance an echo honked back.

Darrell wandered from the garage, working his hands over with a rag.

Richie asked: "You Harlin?"

"Nope. Darrell."

"Harlin around?"

"He's up at the Lookout."

"When's he gonna be back?"

"Ain't gonna be back. He's dead. Lookout's the cemetery."

Richie huffed a laugh. A "fuck you" laugh. "You a comedian? Hey, Tony, this guy's a fucking comedian."

"Joe Piscopo," Tony said.

"Only no muscles, and half the brains," Richie said. "Pump us some gas, funny boy."

Darrell gave a nervous titter. He slid over to the pumps and started filling the Town Car. Richie came up behind him. He blocked out the sun.

Richie said: "We're looking for this place Sierra, funny boy."

"This is it."

Richie took a look around. "Some town," he said.

"Like a New Jersey dump," Tony said.

"Without the good parts," Richie said.

Darrell flustered. "Well . . . town is really down the road a piece."

"It gets better?" Tony asked.

"Like dead fish get fresher," Richie answered.

Tony said: "Dead fish don't stink like this place does."

Another titter from Darrell that said he was trying to be one of the boys. It bought him nothing. Gas came spilling out of the tank onto his overalls. Nervous: "Shit to hell! I didn't . . . I wasn't watching."

Richie peeled some bills off a wad of cash, and jammed them down into Darrell's front pocket. "Tell Uncle Jed to get you another pair just like 'em." He pulled out a pack of cigarettes and jabbed one between his lips. A book of matches twisted through the fingers of his right hand.

"Let me axe you something, funny boy. You see some guy roll through here today? Young, pretty boy, fucked-up hand?"

Darrell hesitated. "Well, I . . . what do you want to know for?"

Richie shook his head remorsefully as if Darrell had just delivered a eulogy. "Funny boy's got questions. Now he's a reporter."

"Peter fucking Jennings," Tony grunted.

The boys had their rhythm going big time now. Like a one-two punch of ginny poetry, all smooth and crazy.

Richie flicked a match lit.

Darrell's hands jerked up. "You shouldn't . . . I got gas on me."

Richie flipped the match at Darrell. If he jumped back an inch it was a mile, and he did it screaming like a bitch. The match fizzled out before it hit him. That made his bitch act all the more pathetic.

Darrell turned to run. Richie's massive hand swallowed him by the shoulder and pulled him back.

Richie had the weary look of a rocket scientist explaining things to a five-year-old. "Now let me axe you again: young, pretty boy, fucked-up hand. You seen him?"

Darrell jerked his head up and down hard. Any harder and he might have snapped it off. "Came in this morning. Went into town, came back, then went to town again." He couldn't sell John out fast enough, but he gave it his best shot. "He's still here."

"How you know?"

"That's his car." Darrell flipped his head toward the Mustang. "Didn't go nowhere without that."

"Maybe he walked somewheres."

"Through the desert? On a day like today? Are you cra—" The mechanic thought better of that one.

Richie let Darrell's shoulder breathe. He peeled off another bill and stuck it where he had stuck the others. "If you're smart, you'll stay stupid."

Darrell nodded, hard like before. Even he didn't need that printed in big type.

The Town Car rocked to one side as Richie lowered himself in. Darrell came to the window.

"This guy you looking for; you gonna . . . there gonna be trouble?"

"More questions," Richie said.

"He's writing a book," Tony said.

"Call it *How I Poked My Nose Where It Don't Belong and Ain't Never Was Heard from Again.*"

"It's just he owes me money. Something happens, then I don't get paid."

The window slid up, banishing Darrell to the other side of tinted glass.

Richie laughed. "Fucking Stewart. What a deadbeat."

Cautiously, John came up on the ticket window of the little bus depot he had so cautiously entered. He wasn't sure what to expect. Sierra was that kind of place.

The clerk asked: "Can I help you, sir?" He asked so fucking normal it was shocking.

"I need a ticket." John's voice was heavy with desperation.

"Where to?"

"Out of here."

". . . But, in particular."

"I . . ." John thought. Someplace far. Someplace safe. Someplace he could disappear. "Mexico. You got a bus that goes to Mexico? That's where I have to go."

"Where in Mexico would you like—"

"I don't care," John snapped. "Just get me out of here."

The clerk harrumphed. He paged through a timetable, holding John in the corner of his eye. "We have a bus to Mexico that arrives in two hours. Has to make a couple of connections, but it will get you across the border."

"How much?"

"One way, or round-trip?"

Coughing a pained laugh: "One way."

The clerk did some figuring. "Thirty even."

From his pocket John pulled what money he had. Twenty-seven dollars. His hand went for another look and found a couple of coins. He held it all up before the clerk in a pathetic gesture. "Twenty-seven fifty. That's all I have."

"The ticket is thirty dollars."

"I bought a beer." John stammered. Thoughts were as hard to catch as butterflies. "I bought a beer. It was two-fifty. I bought it, otherwise I would have thirty."

The clerk herded up all the sympathy he could. "I'm sorry, sir. It's thirty dollars for the ticket."

John moved a little. He swayed the way a battered punching bag sways. "Yeah. A little short. Figures. I just wanted to get out, that's all." The money went back to his pocket.

The clerk had nothing to say, so he said nothing.

John turned, slumped at the shoulders, and slowly shuffled away. He hadn't moved more than a few feet when he suddenly whirled and lunged for the clerk. Grabbing him up by the shirt, John jerked him halfway across the counter.

"Please, you don't understand. I have to get out of here. They're going to come looking for me! They're going to kill me!" Eyes wide and wild. A dog in the street would have been shot for being half as mad. "If I can't get this ticket, then I'm going to do things to get out of here! I don't want to hurt anybody! I just want to leave!" He said it again in a whimper. "I just want to leave."

The clerk tried to wrestle himself free. "I'll give you the money, okay? I'll give you two-fifty. Just . . ." He broke John's grip.

The whole world seemed to grow away from John as if his own shame was diminishing him.

The clerk busted records writing up a ticket, too scared to ever once look directly at the wild man across from him.

"Here." The clerk thrust the ticket forward. He kept at a good arm's length. "Bus two twenty-three. Gets here in two hours."

John turned over the twenty-seven fifty, and took the ticket. A pitiful little voice came out of him. "I'm sorry. It's just . . . the heat."

All that bought him from the clerk was a cold stare.

John headed for the door. He took a few paces and stopped and looked back at the ticket window.

The clerk hung a sign: CLOSED.

Richie and Tony rolled up into the truck stop. Except for Flo and the short-order cook, it was empty. The two men took up seats at the counter, leaving a stool vacant between them. Even at that, it would have been hard to slip a piece of paper through the space where their shoulders met.

Flo brought over a rag and moved around the dirt in front of them. She slid a couple of menus across the counter.

Richie made like he was looking at it. He said: "Hot out."

Flo said: "That's why they call it the desert." She worked her gum. "Want something?"

"I figure a glass of wine would be too much to ask for."

"You can ask for whatever you want. But what you get is what we got."

Richie looked at her over his menu. "Tony, another comedian."

Tony said: "Like the colored chick with the Jew name."

"But this one I can stand to look at," Richie said.

Flo jabbed a pencil behind her ear. "You sure know how to sweet-talk a woman." The words dripped from her lips. "I guess they don't have many ladies where you come from. Or maybe ladies isn't what you boys like." She got cute with a smile. "Tell me something: Which of you watches football while the other does the dishes?"

Richie and Tony let the silence go unbothered.

The Wurlitzer quit a song and started another.

Richie growled a laugh, tossed an elbow to Tony, and pointed at Flo. "This one's funny," he said to Tony. "You're funny," he said to Flo.

"Yeah, I'm hysterical. Good at birthdays, better at weddings. Are you ordering or not?" She didn't miss a beat with her gum.

"Couple of beers. Whatever you got," said Richie. He watched Flo walk over to the cooler. He leaned in over the counter to get a better look. "Not bad."

Tony grunted.

"She'd go for me."

Tony laughed.

"What's the joke? She'd go for me. Women go for me."

"Yeah, women go for you. Twenty dollars a turn. For fifty they love you, and for seventy-five they might not use the same lines twice."

Richie balled his face into a scowl. "You didn't have to go like that."

"Couple hours away from Mr. Vesci, and you go love simple for the first gash you see."

"So I go for a girl? You didn't have to go like that."

Tony made a fist with his right hand and ground it into the palm of his left. "See what it matters to me if you marry her, move a block from nowhere, and she shits kids. But first off we got work. That's all I'm thinking."

Flo came back clutching two beers. She planted them in front of the men and started to write up a tab.

"Say, uh, maybe you can help me out," Richie said. "I'm looking for a friend."

"Sure you are. Someone to talk to, a shoulder to cry on, and maybe, if things work out that way, you'll make me see some fireworks." She didn't look up from writing her check.

Tony sucked at his beer.

Richie smiled. "You're getting ahead of yourself. I'm looking for a guy. Pretty boy, bad hand."

She tore off the check, and let it flutter down to the counter. "Yeah, I seen him this morning. Couldn't tell you where he's at now."

"His car's still around."

"Mister, this town ain't but arm's length. Your friend's still here, then you'd hit him if you closed your eyes and threw a stick."

Flo started away. Richie grabbed her by the wrist, gently as he could, but it was still enough to jerk her back. He said, "Maybe later you and me could go somewhere."

Flo looked over Richie. She looked out the window at the silver Town Car, at the Nevada plates. Nevada, a few miles and a world away. She had been to Nevada once. It wasn't much, but what it wasn't was Sierra. As far as Flo was concerned, as far as any sane person would be, that made it paradise.

Flo gave something like a smile. "Sure we can go somewhere. If somewhere is somewhere out of here."

Flo went into the kitchen. Richie and Tony finished their beers and left.

Richie tipped heavy.

He stood, then sat, then stood again, then lay across a bench, then couldn't stand to not check his watch one more time. Five minutes had passed since the last time John stood, sat, stood again, and checked his watch. Ten minutes down, an hour and fifty minutes to go.

Not so long, he thought. An hour and fifty minutes and he would be free. And how bad could Mexico be? Dirty, maybe, and run-down, but beer was cheap and women were cheaper. It was the kind of place where a couple bucks stretched easy into a party.

The sun crawled closer to the west, to the horizon, to night.

Mexico. It was also the kind of place he could turn a few dollars, send the money back to Mr. Vesci. Maybe throw in some interest. John nodded to himself. Yeah, with cats like Mr. Vesci, a little money could work a lot.

He rubbed at his throat. Dry. He tried to hawk up some saliva but got nothing. Again to the watch: Five more minutes, fifteen altogether, and every one felt like an hour. He looked up in the sky. The sun hung there, stuck.

Down the street and across, the soda machine sat tucked in a corner. John ran his hands over himself and

115

managed to come up with some change. Enough. Maybe. He looked back at the machine: a block away, if that. It seemed far enough to be a day by train.

Picking himself up, he started down the street. Even this late in the day that was enough to break a sweat. John stopped and turned and looked at the bus depot. He looked back toward the soda machine and started for it again. Slowly at first, then faster, propelled by some sudden, unexplained fear, as if leaving the bus depot was as much leaving his only chance at freedom.

John ran, his dry throat wheezing with each breath. His arms and legs pumped hard the length of the block. The soda machine bobbed and came closer. He slowed as he arrived; a safe haven. The wasted fear flooded from his body. He felt stupid for running, for being afraid of nothing. Just the same, he was in a hurry to get the soda and get back to the sanctuary of the bus station.

Something blurred before him. It moved with a low fast violence, and struck him hard in the stomach. John's feet lifted from the ground and he felt bile rush up his throat. The sky and the earth flipped. The ground raced toward him. His good hand took the fall, but his face helped out. The bus ticket flipped from his pocket out into the street.

John clutched at his gut and choked on the burning stomach juices that spilled from his mouth. He rolled over and looked up through watery eyes.

"Get up, mister." Toby Tyler leered down at him. "Don't ever let it be said that Toby Tyler beat the living shit out of somebody without givin' them a fair chance."

"Are you crazy?" John coughed and spat blood. "What the hell are you doing?"

"I'm doing what any man would do if he was offended. Beatin' you up."

John dragged the back of a hand across his mouth. "You stupid punk! You don't even know what you're fighting over!"

"My honor, that's what I'm fighting over. Now get up, or do I have to whoop you where you lie?"

Jenny came flying up the street, her arms swimming through the air as she ran. "Toby," she screamed. "Toby Tyler, leave him alone!"

"You stay away, Jenny. I aim to mess this man up, and that ain't a thing for a woman to see."

Jenny went to her knees. She cradled John's head in her lap, bending his neck at an awkward angle. "Don't be afraid of him none." She stroked his face. "I don't care what he does to you. We can still be together."

John yanked his head from her. "Get away from me." He rubbed his strained neck muscles.

A hot breeze kicked up the ticket in a cartwheel. John pushed up and scrambled for it. Toby was faster.

"Now, what's this?" The boy held it taut between his fingers and twisted it from one side to the other.

"Give it to me!" Words quick and sharp.

"Mexico? You going to Mexico?"

"Yes! I'm leaving. You never have to see me again. Just please, give it to me!"

"This mean something to you?" Toby looked to Jenny. "She means something to me."

The first tear Toby gave the ticket was a slow one. The sound of the separating paper crawled deep into John's head.

John screamed, "NO!"

Toby went at the ticket, long and violently, tearing it again and again. He let the pieces slip from his hands, and they danced in the breeze. They fell before John like a bitter snow.

"I'm going to beat you," Toby said. "Beat you so bad you gonna be eatin' nothing but soup the rest of your days. Rain dogs is going to be prettier than you when I'm done. I'm gonna mess you up so bad you gonna make your own mama sick. I'm gonna . . ."

Toby's voice came to John like a distant sound that drifts through the darkness on a black night. The world didn't just tilt this time, it twisted and churned and bent at an odd angle around him. John could see nothing. He felt nothing. He couldn't feel his fingers curl into a fist, or the fist smashing into Toby's head. Not the first time. Not the third time. Not the seventh time. John had no sensation as Toby's skull became a soft, bloody goo that caked his knuckles and spilled down into the dirt. His arm pumped like a piston again and again into what was left of the boy's face.

Jenny wailed. "Stop it! You're killing him!" She grabbed John by the arm and threw on all her weight. "You're killing him!"

John's arm slowed from exhaustion, his chest heaved.

The girl sank to the ground. She took Toby's oozing head in her hands. "Toby?"

The boy gurgled blood.

Jenny wept over him, and gently murmured his name.

John watched her cry. He watched the blood bubble from the side of Toby's face. He looked down at his own hand, his knuckles dripped a red sweat.

For a long moment it looked like someone else's hand;

bloody, vicious, cruel. Slowly he recognized it as his own. John backed away. He caught himself on his own feet and stumbled as he turned and broke into a dead run. Nowhere to go. No way to get there.

All of a sudden John's doing a Warner Brothers cartoon skid to a dead stop. And lookit why: A silver Town Car turned into his path. It crept toward him, close enough that John could see the hulking figure behind the wheel. Phantom pain ate at his left hand.

John turned and raced back the way he came. Behind him he could hear the growl of tires as they bit into the dirt and sent the Town Car racing forward.

Tight around a corner John headed behind a building and over a fence. He ran until he dropped into the dirt, his legs still trying to kick him forward. He lay there too weak to move—straining to hear over the short, raspy breaths he sucked—waiting for a bullet in the back of the head.

It never came.

No sound.

No movement.

After a long while John got his legs under him and stood. He walked, slowly, cautiously, trying to remember where the phone booth was.

"Holy shit!" Richie hit the brakes and the Town Car jerked to a stop.

Tony slid into the dashboard. The seat belt wouldn't fit around him. "What the hell are you doing?"

Richie pointed a beefy finger beyond the windshield.

"That's him. That's that fuck Stewart."

119

"Then what the fuck did you stop for?" Tony worked himself back into the seat. "You should've run him the fuck over."

Outside, on the street, John wheeled and ran.

"Fucker!" Richie jammed the accelerator. The back end of the Town Car sank as its tires dug into the dirt and launched the car forward. It bore down on John, lost him as he ducked down a side street, backed and followed.

John disappeared between two buildings. Richie shot across a street, wrenched hard on the wheel, and fishtailed the Town Car around a corner. Lights flashed in the rearview mirror. Red and blue. Richie screwed his neck and looked over his shoulder. "Sheriff" was painted in big black letters on the car behind him.

"Shit." Tony's head twisted side to side. "We don't need this."

"I'll handle it."

"If we're going to deal with this Stewart guy, we can't have trouble. Cop, or not."

Sheriff Potter followed his stomach up out of the police car and began a slow mosey toward the two men.

Richie slipped a snub-nosed .38 from his shoulder holster and made it vanish under his thigh. "I'll handle it."

The Sierra phone book was more like a phone pamphlet. The third name under the Ms was McKenna. John let his last bit of change slip into the pay phone. It would have gone for a soda to drink while he waited for his bus to Mexico if Toby hadn't started something.

If Jenny would have left him alone.

If Richie hadn't rolled into town.

If . . .

Possibility gave way to reality. Grace answered the phone. "Hello," she said, as regular as any woman who didn't want her husband dead.

"Grace, it's John."

There was a quiet rustle on the other end of the line like someone moving through a room. A door closed, then Grace said, "Thought you would be on your way to Vegas by now. Is there something you wanted?"

"I wanted to talk." He read the line casual, old chums just catching up.

"I don't think we have anything to talk about."

"What about us?"

Quiet.

Then: "There is no us, remember?"

"Except I can't get you out of my mind. I've thought about you every second since I left there. I can still taste you on my lips."

"Stop it."

"Why? Am I making you hot, or does the truth scare you?"

She could feel his Cheshire grin across the wire. "Because I know you're full of shit."

"I mean it, Grace. I want to take you with me."

"I thought you couldn't leave? I thought you couldn't get your car?"

John eased his words out. "I could if I had Jake's money."

The woman went cold. "Is that what changed your mind? The money?"

"I don't give a fuck about the money. I want you, and I want to get out of this hellhole. There's only one way to do that."

She thought about it. "Are you sure? About me, I mean."

"I came back for you this morning, Grace. Before I even knew about the money, I came back. You're what I want."

Grace was silent.

John said, "The only reason I stormed off is because you spooked me talking about killing Jake. But that just gave me time to think, and it keeps coming back to you and me and us getting out of here." He hauled in a deep breath and brought it home. "But we've got to get the money, baby. We get the money, I get the car, then we get the hell out."

"You said you couldn't kill anybody."

"We don't have to kill him. Just knock him out, and tie him up till we get away."

Across the line John heard a fingernail snapping between teeth.

"Grace? It was your idea, remember? I'm doing this for you. I'm doing this so you can fly."

The silence kept coming.

Come on, come on, John thought. She's the one wanted Jake dead. Now when he was offering it up, why'd it take a hard sell?

There came a quick breath: "After dark. I'll leave the back door open."

A click. A dial tone.

John hung up the phone. He sucked his lips back against his teeth. It looked like a smile.

Grace turned the phone off. With the butt of her hand she pressed the antenna down into the handset. She took a moment—a moment to gather herself, and look like everything in the world was the same as before she answered the phone—then opened the kitchen door and went back into the living room.

Jake was sunk into an easy chair, head obscured by a newspaper. Pipe smoke belched over the top, and collected in a brown cloud. It hung over him same as Los Angeles air on a halfway decent day.

Grace leaned against the wall; body stiff, arms crossed.

Jake's headless body grumbled. "Who was on the phone?"

"Wrong number."

A spew of smoke, then: "You spent a long time talking for a wrong number. But then you make friends so easily, don't ya, Grace?"

Grace let it pass. "Jake?"

From behind the paper came some kind of sound.

"I put up new drapes, Jake."

"I know that. I was here when you was tutoring yer apprentice."

"You never said anything."

"About the drapes, or about yer apprentice?"

Grace chewed her tongue for a second. "The drapes."

"Sure, and they look fine."

"You haven't even looked at them yet."

The paper folded. Jake looked at the windows, eyes empty like a fish laid out at market. He disappeared behind the paper again. "They look fine."

She stared at Jake. Grace thought of what he looked like behind the paper. She thought of the chain that hung from his neck. She thought of the key that dangled from the end of the chain.

The paper dropped. Grace had stared too hard, and he had felt her. "What the hell are you looking at, girl?"

Grace worked to keep her voice steady. "Nothing, Jake. Absolutely nothing."

The sun hit the horizon and exploded. The sky lit in a red-orange blaze. The air cooled, and soothed; a gentle hand caressing worn souls.

"Well, that's it. The sun's going down." The old blind man still sat on the corner. His best friend still lay next to him. Flies buzzed. "People go home, trade stories over dinner. They'll talk about the day, about the heat, laugh about something crazy it made them do. They'll kiss, sleep a few hours, then do it all over again."

John said, "The day wasn't that bad. We all got through it all right."

The old man laughed sharp and quick. "Day ain't over yet. Night is part of day. Same twenty-four hours. Separate, but equal. Night is when you let your guard down; when you see things in the shadows, and hear things in the dark."

"You're a hell of a pessimist, old man." John's eyes swept the streets. Nothing. At least no Town Car.

"Night is when you want to sleep, but the dry heat and a strange noise keeps you tossin' and turnin'. It's when you wish the sun was bakin' high in the sky so you could see just what it was you're afraid of."

John stared back at himself in the old man's dark glasses. "Are you afraid of the dark?"

"Afraid of it? Boy, I live in darkness. People are afraid of what they can't see. I can't see nothin', so it's all the same to me. A peck on the cheek from a beautiful girl, a lick from a dog, the kiss of death. It's all the same to me."

"You don't fear death?"

The old man's head shook. "We was born to die, boy. From the minute you take your first breath, you've got a death sentence hangin' over you. You just don't know where, or when, or how. Don't make sense worryin' about the particulars."

John watched the night slowly fizzle out the sun. "We're all just floating along like twigs in a stream, so enjoy the ride. Is that it?"

The old man turned down the corners of his mouth. "More or less."

"Not this twig, friend. I got plans."

Again the short, quick laugh. "We all got plans. I planned on seeing all my days. I know you didn't plan on straying into this town. Sometimes life don't give a good god-damn what we was planning."

"No, I guess it doesn't. But I'll tell you one thing I'm not planning on, and that's sticking around." He got up from the corner. "Don't figure I'll be seeing you again. Take it easy, old man."

The old man turned his head in John's direction. "Same back at you."

"Any parting words of wisdom?"

He nodded. "Things ain't always what they seem." The old man spoke like he was teaching science. "You got to ask yourself: Is it worth it?"

The words chilled; ice water on John's spine. His jaw skipped side to side. "You talk too much, old man."

John flipped a coin into the old man's tin cup. He headed toward the edge of town, toward Grace, looking over his shoulder for a Town Car as he went.

The old man waited a few moments before sliding his sunglasses down his nose. He dug into the tin cup after John's coin and held it up to the fading light. A quarter. His eyes squinted angrily after John. A full day of spouting bullshit for a fucking quarter?

"Cheap bastard," he spat.

The old man woke up his dog and headed home.

Grace stood by the back door of the house staring at the dead bolt as if it were in mid-conversation.

From somewhere in the house Jake yelled. "What are ya doing, girl? Are ya comin' to bed, or aren't ya?"

Grace's hand wavered. Up, then back, then suddenly, finally, it struck at the lock the way a snake goes for a field mouse.

"I'm coming, Jake."

Turning out the lights, she hurried into the darkness.

In the bedroom window, silhouettes moved back and forth in an unrehearsed and sloppy dance. John stood, away, in the sagebrush, watching and chanting. "Come on, come on."

After a time the lights went out.

John waited, moonlight strong enough to read his watch by. He lit a cig, and had himself a smoke.

Eight minutes. Eleven. Thirteen.

He stamped out the smoke, then had another. The night crawled like the day. How long did it take a man to fall asleep? A man like Jake? A man who could stomach lunch while his wife was supposedly being killed?

Twenty minutes.

For some reason John caught himself thinking of Gayle. He wasn't sure why, but figured it was because of the night probably. It was cool, like the cool evenings after a Vegas scorcher when he used to walk Gayle from the casino back to their house. Her house. The one he split the rent on. Sometimes.

He would have driven her, but she liked to walk at night. John was never big on the idea of letting her go it alone because it was dangerous, and she might get hurt, and because he . . . he cared about her.

A little laugh.

Yeah. He cared about her. In all the wild, juiced-up craziness that had been going on since his forced departure, John had forgotten that little item. Hell, he'd forgotten it a long time ago. Eight months he'd been with Gayle, and in eight months she'd become just a chick who had a roof he could crash under, a decent lay when he got up the energy or wasn't worn-out from fucking somebody else, and mostly, she had become a reliable source of cash when things got tight.

But she hadn't always been just that. When he had first met her she had been beautiful and sweet and kind. She always was beautiful and sweet and kind. But in time a man forgets such insignificant things as a woman's gentle looks and tender words. How? John wondered. And why is it a man only remembers these things when it's far too late, having been distracted by some other woman's not-much-better looks, and pretty-much-the-same words.

It was a universal constant: For every chick everywhere, no matter how lovely, or smart, or good, there was a guy who'd forgotten that and fucked things up with her. It was small comfort to John knowing he wasn't alone in the world.

He thought, too, of something Gayle had said to him: that she had wasted eight months. He was too scared of getting himself killed to even consider what she was babbling about before.

He got it now.

He got how he had stolen two hundred forty days—two thirds of a year—of her life, of her youth, of her essence and her soul. Steal money, and you can pay it back. Steal a car, you can buy someone a new one. You can't pay back stolen time. There's no reimbursing a life interrupted.

John felt like . . . he felt like shit. He felt remorse, and guilt, and a whole bunch of other stuff that reminded him—for the first time in a long time—he was a human being. And in its own far-out way, that felt good.

He got over it.

Stamping out his smoke, John moved on the house.

The back door, a gentle twist of the knob, not even a creak as it opened. John slipped in like a morning mist. Pitch-black; no moonlight inside. He walked like the blind, hands before him, repeating the same motion over and over: edging a leg forward and his body following. Edging a leg forward and his body following. It was slow going across the room.

He stepped, his shin hit the edge of a table. In the quiet, the dull crack of bone and wood was like a gunshot. A lamp faltered, tipped from the tabletop. He grabbed in the dark, the lamp brushed the floor, but didn't break.

John stood hunched over, lamp in hand. He didn't move. Every breath sounded like a hurricane.

Jake stirred.

"Jake, what's the matter?" Grace tried to throw some sleep in her voice, but she just came off sounding like Elmer Fudd.

"Ya didn't hear somethin'?"

"I was sleeping." She rubbed at her eyes as if to prove it.

Jake's head jerked from side to side, trying to catch sound. "There's someone in the house."

"I don't hear anything." A hand to Jake's chest. It brushed the key. "You were dreaming. Or maybe the wind blew something over."

"The wind isn't blowing."

Jake's hand slipped into the nightstand drawer. When it came out, an extra finger glinted in the moonlight.

"Jake, what is that?"

"What does it look like?" His wet teeth shown in the dark.

"Jake, when did you buy a gun?"

He slid from the covers and moved toward the bedroom door.

Grace went for his arm. "Oh my God, Jake. No. If it is someone, they'll go away. Or call the sheriff. Don't go out there."

"What are you afraid of? I'm the one's got the gun."

Jake tossed her off. He went out the door and was swallowed by the dark.

———

John baby-stepped through the house. He tried to remember it: the living room where he hung drapes led to the hall, to the bathroom where he showered, to the bedroom where he fucked Grace. He thought about that part, about fucking Grace. Fear kept him from going hard. He made out a doorway, groped for it, through it.

Something cold and hard pressed into the center of his forehead and pushed him back into the room. The lights flashed on bright and blinding. John's eyes crept back open. Jake stood on the good end of an automatic.

"Well, well," Jake cooed. "As I live. Didn't expect to see the likes of you again. Thought you'd be long on yer way by now."

"Yeah, well . . ." John's eyes were filled with the metal of the gun. "Me, too."

"More troubles with the car?"

"You could say. I don't even have it yet."

"Darrell giving you problems?"

John wanted to laugh, just standing there chatting with Jake like two women at tea. Funny as hell, except for the gun. "He did more work on the car. He wants fifty bucks extra for it."

Jake made a thinking face. "Fifty dollars more. That's a lot of money, especially when you don't have a dime. And where did you plan on getting the money from? Maybe you thought you'd pay yer old friend Jake a visit."

John felt his bowels loosen. "It's not like that."

"Maybe you heard old Jake's got some money stashed away, and you'd help yerself to a little."

"Wait a minute, Jake. Just listen to me."

"You thought you'd come in here in the middle of the night and wham! Wail off and clock old Jake McKenna and turn his brains into wallpaper."

"Jake—!"

The automatic bored into John's forehead. He back-pedaled. The gun stayed with him.

Jake went on him like a man possessed. "And then with Jake out of the way, you could borrow yer two hundred dollars. Or maybe two thousand. Or maybe twenty thousand. Who's to stop you? Not ol' Jake. Sure, Jake would be dead."

"That's not the reason I came. I swear."

Amused: "There's another reason? It better be good."

"I came for Grace."

Jake's head pulled sideways. "You came to take my wife from me?"

Quick and to the point John said, "I came to kill her."

"Liar."

"It's the truth."

"That's a thick change of heart."

"Yeah, well, a couple of hours ago I just about killed a guy over a girl. Not for money, for a girl. And she was just going to stand there and let it happen. Or let him kill me. The same way Grace was going to let us beat the shit out of each other." The muscles in his jaw went stiff. His words shot fast and hard. "I don't like that, Jake. Not twice in one day. And maybe I'm so hot and bothered and pissed I'd twist the neck off my own grandma to get out of here."

John could feel Jake's sneer across the length of the gun.

"That's talk. A whole lot of talk."

"Dammit, Jake. There're two guys on the streets right

now gunning for me. If I don't get out, I go down. And if the choice is between me and Grace, then I vote for Grace."

John went smooth and steady; a door-to-door salesman closing for the kill. "You were going to pay me thirteen thousand. Give me two hundred, I'll kill her and dump the body where bloodhounds won't find her.

"But I need the money, Jake. I have to have it."

Jake figured things out. He took his time about it, like Grace would keep. She would.

In the desert a coyote bayed. Nothing answered.

Jake eased back the gun. It left a small red circle in the middle of John's forehead. Like a target.

"She's in the bedroom," Jake whispered. His voice was lightly frosted with regret.

John looked down at the automatic in Jake's hand. He didn't hesitate. He went straight for the hall to the bedroom.

"Hold a second." Jake beckoned John back.

John went.

"I'm wondering something." The barrel of the automatic slid up and down on Jake's temple as if it was trying to rub a thought loose. "I'm wondering just how is it you happen to know where the bedroom's at."

"Wha . . ." Words got all jumbled up in John's throat. "What are you talking about?"

"This morning when I came in on you and the missus, you told me you hadn't so much as been near the bedroom. Now you make straight for it."

John huffed air and tried to make it pass for a laugh. "Come on, Jake—"

Jake swung up the gun, his thumb jammed back the hammer. John paid attention.

"Don't 'Jake' me, boy. It's a big house. Any of these

halls could lead to the bedroom. Odd you know yer way. Excepting maybe you've been in there before. Maybe with Grace to mind you some attention."

"Nothing happened with me and Grace this morning."

"Then maybe this afternoon. When I sent you to kill my wife you end up sexing her instead."

"For God's sake—" The barrel of the gun came hard up into John's throat, choking him off.

"Is that what happened? Did you even make it to the desert, or did you just ply the afternoon between my sheets?"

"You're not talking sense." The words gurgled from him.

"If I had any sense, I'd have killed you this morning and been done with it."

"What are you ... you can't ... you can't kill me." John's flesh went white against the dark.

"A drifter, a loner, a troublemaker like you? Yer trespassing, lad. A man's got to protect his home, his wife. Face it; yer dead, and not even yer own mother would say anything against it."

"Okay, okay! What difference does it make if I slept with Grace? You don't care about her."

"Yer right. I don't give a damn about Grace. But to screw a man's wife behind his back? You won't be making a fool of me, laddie."

Jake drew down. He could barely make out the fading red circle in John's forehead. Barely, but good enough.

In one breath: "Killing me's the wrong move. Grace is the one you have to worry about." He sucked air and went again. "She wants you dead. She wants you dead, and she wants your money."

"What are you prattling about?"

"How plain do I have to make it? Think about it: How'd I get in here? You hear glass break, or a door splinter?"

Jake's arm bent at the elbow. The gun pointed away from John as much as it pointed at him. Things could go either way.

"How did the evening end, Jake? After you went to bed, did she linger for a few minutes? Maybe just long enough to unlatch the back door? Is that what happened?"

Jake's head kicked back and his face shattered into a million pieces. It took him a while to put it back together. "You'd tell me anything to save yer pathetic life."

John poured it on. Easy, not too hard. "You're kidding yourself, Jake. You know what kind of woman Grace is. She'd do anything to get out of here. What makes you think when you were planning to kill her, she wasn't doing the same for you?"

John's voice went warm, as if he could have been talking sports or barbecuing but just happened to be talking murder.

"What's she to you, Jake; a woman who'd have you dead? Let me do her." He said it the way you ask a favor. "All I want is two hundred dollars to get out of here with."

"Two hundred dollars?"

"And you pocket fifty thousand to spend as you please."

The automatic seemed to float for a long while in the air. It bobbed, up and down, side to side, as if unsure of where to go. Finally it swung away from John.

John began a smile. His lips never made more than a grin before the gun flew back, hard, against the side of his head.

Darkness exploded all around John. He hurled backward a hundred miles before his back crushed up against a wall. Another hundred miles, and he hit the floor. His mouth filled with the blood that ran from his head.

John's eyes fluttered, and he saw the gun float toward him. There was that black eye of death staring at him one more time.

In Jake's voice the eye said, "I don't think we can do business. Killing my wife for me; that's one thing. Fucking her's another."

The hammer went back on the automatic. It was loud in John's ear, sounding like a felled redwood tearing from its stump. He slammed shut his eyes and waited for the explosion of the bullet from the chamber. What came was a scream.

"Jake, no!"

Jake spun toward the voice; Grace in the doorway. He turned his back to John for a split second that dragged on for an eternity.

John moved. Without thought, without plan, but as sure as his life depended on it, he moved for Jake. He pulled a forearm across Jake's throat and a hand clawed at the gun.

Jake fought the way a wild bull fights a rider. He twisted and bucked and leaped under John's grip, but his size and strength gave him no advantage.

The gun barked and fired a bright red orange. Across the room a framed picture of Jake and Grace took the bullet. The glass shattered and fell to the floor a crystal rain. In the picture a violent wound separated Jake from his wife.

John worked the gun loose. Clank-clank, it hit the floor.

Grace's hands gripped hard at the doorway as she watched the two men perform their dance of death. She might as well have been watching a movie. She felt the same detached excitement, the same vicarious thrill. But the fear Grace felt—the fear of impending death, and whose it might be—was real. Still, even that only made the watching all the more exhilarating.

John's arm strained and wrenched at Jake's neck until the older man slowed. He dropped to one knee, but fought on as if only retreating to lower ground.

John stayed with him, riding Jake as he went down to a second knee and steadied himself with first one arm, then the other.

Jake's breath came in raspy gurgles. His eyes swelled in their sockets and his tongue filled his mouth. He looked up at Grace, his face twisted in fear and confusion.

Grace looked back. Cold, distant.

A dull, dead thud as Jake's head bounced against the floor. John kept choking, and choking, and choking long after Jake was dead. Finally he fell back from the body, panting, wet, and shaking. Eyes narrowed, he looked to Grace.

"Why the hell didn't you do anything?"

"What was I supposed to do?"

"You could have hit him, or kneed him in the balls." He grabbed up Jake's gun from the floor. "You could have shot him."

"And maybe shot you by accident."

A thought came to John. The very idea of it made him sick in the stomach. "You liked watching that, didn't you? You got off on it."

Grace started to say something. The chain around Jake's red and black-and-blue neck caught her eye.

"The money!"

Grace lunged for the chain and pulled it free, key and all, as respectful of Jake's body as she would be to driftwood.

"Where's the safe?"

"I don't know."

John coughed air same as if he'd just taken a shot to the body. "You don't know? Jesus Christ! Don't you think we should have found out before we killed Jake?"

"I know where it is, I . . . I just don't know exactly where." She went a long way to sound reasonable. "I never saw the safe. I just heard Jake talk about it."

John laughed. "That's rich. We kill Jake because you heard him talk about some money that you've never seen. That's fucking brilliant!"

"Don't yell at me!"

Grace went to a wall and pressed herself flat against it. Head down, she counted out six steps, turned to her left, and counted out three more. She pointed at the floor.

"Right here. Six steps out, three steps left. That's what I heard him say."

John went to the spot beneath Grace's fingers and clawed at the floorboards the way a starving animal goes for food. He tore his fingertips raw against the wood. The floorboards gave nothing. "Go get a knife or something."

Grace was sucked up by the dark, then reappeared knife in hand. John grabbed it from her, then worked it between the wood. The knife slipped loose a few times, cutting him once, before it finally took hold.

"I got it! It's coming!"

A panel broke free. John pulled at another one until it splintered and gave. With wild eyes he looked down into the hole he had torn. Inside was just more floor.

"Nothing. There's no safe under here."

"There has to be!"

"There isn't! There's nothing here, Grace! Jesus fucking Christ! We killed a man for nothing!"

Grace went to the floor beside him. She ripped at the wood frantically, made the hole larger, but it stayed empty. "It's got to be here. I heard him talk about it. He bragged about it. Six steps out, three left."

John sat back. He let himself have a laugh. "This is good, real good. This is so good they might not even send us up for murder when they catch us. They'll probably just lock us up for being idiots."

"If it isn't here, why would he wear that stupid key?"

"You're calling Jake stupid? You?"

"I told you not to yell at me!" The words flew from Grace's mouth mixed with spittle. "I know it's here, dammit! I know it!"

John's eyes went soft. "Wait. Wait a second." Up to his feet, he went quickly to the spot at the wall where Grace had counted out her steps.

"Jake's taller than you." John paced off six steps. "His steps are going to be bigger." He turned, counted three more. He stood a couple of feet from where they had been digging. John's legs went out from under him. He dropped to the floor and pulled hard at the wood.

"Here." Grace gave him the knife. John wedged it between two floorboards and pried one free, then another. He looked down at a small door, steel, a keyhole in the center and a handle to the side.

John stuck out his hand. "The key!"

Grace slapped the key into his palm. John worked the lock, pulled open the door, and dropped his arm down. A slapping sound echoed from inside the safe as his hand hit up against the sides. He stopped, drew his arm out. Money, stiff green bills, seeped between his fingers.

"Look at it all, Grace."

She looked.

John tossed the money on the floor and pulled out another fistful. "There's a hundred thousand in there, easy. More than that."

Grace went all happy. A little girl at Christmas. "I told you. I knew it was there." She scooped up the money and washed herself in it. "Didn't I tell you?"

She fell into John. She kissed him on the neck and cheeks, then hard on the lips. "We'll split it right down the middle. Fifty-fifty. You don't have to take me with you. You can go your own way if you want."

Grace pressed her lips to his. Her tongue wagged in his mouth like a cocker spaniel's tail.

"If you want," she said once more.

John ran his hands over her breasts. Her nipples poked at his palms. "We're going all the way. Together."

She kissed him again, like before, only better.

John said, "Let's go in the bedroom."

"No." With a sweep of her hand Grace spread the money across the floor, fashioning a blanket. She went down, and took John down with her. "Let's do it here."

"What about . . . what about him?" John jerked his head toward the body on the floor. Jake looked on with cold, empty, bloated eyes. He still looked confused.

Grace smiled. "Let him watch. I want him to know what he's missing."

Grace kissed John. She kissed him, she bit him, she licked and pulled at him. Grace put her body to his wherever she could, any way she could think of.

John was slow to start, but like the dry brush he couldn't help catch fire.

ohn sat up. Money clung to his naked, sweaty back. From somewhere in the darkness next to him, Grace reached up and peeled away the bills.

He pulled on a shirt and dressed himself. Grace stayed on the floor, wrapped in shadow. "Now what?"

"You got a suitcase?"

"Never needed one. I've never been anywhere. I've got a backpack."

"Get it, and put all the money in it. Pack up anything else you want to take with you." John picked up two bills from the floor. Two hundred dollars. He fastened his pants as he moved for the door.

"Where are you going?"

"To get my car."

"Wait. What about . . ." She didn't know if she should say Jake's name, or point, or what. Finally she uncurled a finger toward the body. "Him."

"Put some clothes on him. When I get back we'll load him in the trunk and dump him in the desert. It'll take days for anybody to find him."

John went out into the night. For a while Grace stared

at her dead husband and thought of nothing. She saw his gun lying on the floor.

She smiled.

John started down the drive past Grace's Jeep. He stopped and thought and walked back. Carefully, quietly popping the hood, he reached in and yanked free a tangle of wires, then tore loose some more for good measure. Just as quietly he closed the hood and walked on.

The walk to Harlin's, to Darrell's, took John into the second part of an hour and half. He was slowed by the dark, and small things that moved and slithered across the road before him.

John was tired, but it was the kind of tired that sleep would cure. If he could sleep. Adrenaline still ran hot in his veins. How long ago had it been since he first rolled into town? Since he'd gone round and round with Darrell, beaten Toby, and seen thirteen thousand dollars end up a swirl of buckshot and blood? If it was an hour ago, it might as well be a month. A year.

And Jake? How long had it been since he felt the old man's throat pressed beneath his forearm, and his windpipe crack? Minutes, but it seemed like something remembered from a high-school play; a vivid, distant memory of something performed but unreal. He reached a hand in his pocket and the two hundred dollars crunched against his fingers. It was no play. What had happened was undeniable.

John felt—here in the dark, alone on the road anyway—no shame for what he had done. No guilt.

What does it take to kill a man? he wondered. He told Jake he wasn't a murderer. And he wasn't. Not when he first got to Sierra. So, what made him kill? Desperation? A heat fever? A chick like Grace, and a hundred thousand dollars? Doesn't take much for even a decent man to do the wrong thing for the right woman.

Maybe that was it.

Or maybe Jake was right. Maybe John had it in him all the time.

What did it take to kill a man? When you get down to it, not much. Just one good try.

The garage was black and quiet when John got to it. Around the side was a little house, a shack. He went to the door and banged a fist on it, waited a few seconds, and banged again. A light went on at the window. A voice poured out from behind the door that sounded the way gravel does on aluminum siding.

"What you want?"

"Open up!"

"We're closed. Come back in the morning."

"It *is* morning."

"Come back when the sun's up."

The light went out.

John pounded on the door, kicked at it.

The light went back on and the door flew open. Darrell stood there shirtless. His hair looked to have been combed with a blender. "What in the hell . . . oh, it's you. Might've figured. What you want?"

"I want my car."

Darrell rubbed hard at his chin. "You got money?"

John pulled the money from his pocket. Darrell's eyebrows did backflips.

"Two hundred dollars in hundred-dollar bills. And this morning you was broke."

"What's it to you?"

"I don't want no dirty money. I run an honest business."

"Yeah, honest like Al Capone on tax day." John grabbed Darrell's hand and pressed the bills hard into his palm. "Where are my keys?"

Darrell fingered the money as if he had something to think about; as if maybe he had to consult with what honesty he had left. He didn't do a lot of soul-searching before dropping back into the shack and returning with John's keys. He tossed them over.

"I think you know where to find it."

John started for the garage.

"By the way."

John stopped and turned back.

"I topped off the tank for you. No charge. Just my friendly way of doing business."

Darrell held up the money next to his crooked, blackened-tooth smile. He laughed as he closed the door on John.

John got his Mustang and drove.

The Mustang turned up the drive to the McKenna house. The headlights broke the dark and landed on nothing. The house was still and silent, the way John left it. Just the way, but not quite.

Something was wrong.

He felt himself go nervous. His stomach fluttered, and a single bead of sweat ran from under his arm along the side of his body. John jammed on the brakes and got out of the car. He stood there looking at the house.

Something was wrong. Something was out of place. Something . . .

Then he realized what it was: nothing. Nothing there. Nothing is where the Jeep had been parked.

"Dammit," he screamed at the night. "Goddamn her! I knew she was going to do this to me." His thoughts tumbled fast. He should have pulled more wires. He should have taken her with him. He should have taken the money. He should have—

The front door opened. Grace yelled in a whisper. "John! What the hell's the matter with you?"

"I . . ."

Grace walked to him. It gave him time to think.

"I just stubbed my toe on a rock. Hurt like hell, that's all."

"I got the money all packed up. I put the Jeep in the garage. Figure that way people will think maybe me and Jake went away. Might buy us some time."

"Yeah. Good thinking."

"Had to push it in. Wouldn't start. Funny thing." She watched John's face. She looked for something that would flare and die as quickly as a struck match. Something that would betray him.

He gave her nothing. "Funny thing," he said.

Jake was dressed like he was going to work, except that he wouldn't be going to work. Or anywhere else. Ever. The body was heavy. It was starting to go stiff, but not so much so it didn't flop around while John and Grace tried to work it through the doors and out of the house. At first they were respectful, but that wore off as they got winded. Finally they figured if Jake could take a few knocks when he was alive, he could sure take them now.

They got him outside, to the car, then lifted the body over the lip of the trunk and tumbled it in. Jake was a tall man. It was a tight fit.

John looked down at the body, folded up unnaturally. Jake didn't look uncomfortable, he just looked like he still didn't get it.

John slammed the trunk closed.

The Mustang rode alone. No other cars on the road. No animals. Nothing. Top down, the rush of air lifted Grace's hair and made it dance behind her. Eyes squinted, she looked hard through the car's windshield.

"I can't see it."

"It should be just up ahead." A beat. "There it is."

The Mustang's headlights caught a sign: YOU ARE LEAVING SIERRA. THANKS FOR VISITING.

Grace howled at the moon. "Oh, God! I'm out! I can't believe it. I'm finally out."

She threw her arms around John's neck and shoulders and kissed his face.

Blinded by her, John swerved. The Mustang dipped hard and cut toward the soft shoulder. John fought it back up onto the blacktop. "Back off! You want to get us killed?"

"I'm sorry. You just don't know how good it is to be free of that place."

"I don't know about that."

"You spent a day in Sierra. I spent almost my entire life there. I feel like someone just took a deadweight off my chest. I feel like I can breathe."

John gave a quick look back at the trunk. "We've still got some deadweight to get rid of."

"Can't we just dump him anywhere?"

"I want to drive out a ways. Pick a spot where no one will find him. Not for a while anyways. Don't worry, it'll be over soon. Then you'll be free."

Grace ran sharp nails down John's neck. "Will you take me with you on your friend's boat?"

"I'm not sailing his boat."

"But you said—"

"We're going to buy a boat of our own, and sail it wherever we want to go."

"Anywhere?"

"What the hell? Anywhere. Where should we go?"

Grace tossed up her hair and let it catch the wind. "Hawai'i. I've read all about it. I've dreamed of going there and just lying on the beach while the water licked up against my feet. God, I'd kill to go there."

With a sideways glance: "You already have."

She looked at John with nothing in her eyes.

Something flashed on the windshield: red, then quickly blue. Grace turned to it. Her face fell apart. "Oh my God!"

Up the road a police car blocked their lane. Sheriff Potter stood before it, flashlight in hand, and waved the Mustang to the side of the road.

"He knows, John." Grace's words were a gasp of fear. "He knows."

"He doesn't know anything. He couldn't."

"What are we going to do?"

"Just shut up. Don't say anything."

Grace's fingers sank into John's arm until they found bone. "I can't go to jail. I couldn't take it."

"Shut up!" John said it hard enough to slap her quiet. "Let me do the talking. He doesn't know anything."

He angled for the shoulder and braked. Sheriff Potter came to the car, his flashlight bright in John's eyes.

"Hello, mister. John, wasn't it?"

"Yes." John held a hand to his eyes.

The circle of light slid from his face to Grace's. "Mrs. McKenna."

Grace didn't speak. She didn't move.

The sheriff pointed the light on the ground. "Nice night for a drive. Morning really. I guess that's about the only way to keep cool; riding around with the top down on a fancy convertible in the first hours of the day." Sheriff Potter stepped on the circle of light at his feet as if it were a bug to be squashed.

Grace snaked a hand to John's.

John said, "Not taking a drive, Sheriff. I'm heading out of town."

Sheriff Potter nodded. "I guess you've had all you can of Sierra. What with that ruckus you had with Toby. Oh, yes. I heard about that."

"Sheriff, he didn't give me any choice. I was just defending—"

"Now just cool down, boy. I ain't accusing you of anything. Serves Toby right to get his ass whooped. If you hadn't done it, somebody else would of."

John craned his neck and tried to look past the police car. "Is there a problem up the road?"

"Nope. No problems up the road." The sheriff brought up the flashlight and let it drift over the backseat of the car. "That your backpack, Mrs. McKenna?"

Grace's hand snapped into a fist, bending back John's fingers. "Yes. Yes it is."

"Taking a little trip?"

"I had a fight with Jake. I just wanted to get away for a few days." Scared as she was, Grace said it all without a moment's hesitation, without so much as a misspoken word. Calm and cool. Honest and real.

John got wise: Lies came naturally to Grace, and this one flowed like melting snow into a river.

She lied on: "Mr. Stewart was kind enough to take me as far as Montrose. I'm going to take a bus to my sister's. I thought I'd stay with her a few days."

"Is that right?" Sheriff Potter sounded interested. He sounded like he bought it. "Can't say as I blame you for wanting to get away for a while. I know I had my fill of Sierra. Sixteen years I've been sheriff here. So long I forgot why I ever wanted the job."

He shined the flashlight out into the brush like he was trying to find something in the lonely dark.

"I guess I became sheriff to help people; keep the peace. Problem is there's so much peace around here there isn't hardly anything for a man to do."

The sheriff paused, as if John or Grace should have something to say at this point.

They didn't.

He went on.

"Got a lot of speeders around here, but they're speeding through miles of nothing, so I can't hardly hold it against them.

"Other than that, well, there ain't much to steal. I figure the last big crime we had here was . . . what would you say, Mrs. McKenna?" Eyes dead on her. "A murder?"

Grace's mouth opened. "I . . ." was all she could come
up with.

"Why don't you step out of the car, mister?"

John did his best to look like he didn't understand what
was going on. For good measure he said: "I don't understand
what's going on."

"Just step from the car, please. Nice and slow."

John timed his wait just long enough to look indignant,
but still cooperative. "Sure, Sheriff."

He pried his hand from Grace's and got out of the Mustang in no particular rush, as if moving slow would somehow
hide his nervousness.

With the flashlight the sheriff traced a line to the Mustang's rear. "Now step around to the back of the car and open
the trunk for me."

John laughed a little laugh that said he had never heard
anything so queer. "What for?"

"Just please do as I say."

"There's nothing in the trunk, Sheriff."

"And as soon as I see that, you're on your way."

Grace's voice came faint the way a night breeze blows
almost unheard. "John—"

"Grace!" Softer: "Just let me handle this. Look, Sheriff,
I'm telling you there's nothing in the trunk." John kept himself calm. No more excited than a man selling appliances. "If
that's not good enough for you, then I'd be happy to open it."
A friendly smile, then the kicker. "Just as soon as you get
yourself a search warrant."

"I could do that. 'Course we'd have to go back into
town. There'd be a whole crowd of people around when the
trunk was opened. A whole crowd of witnesses. And that
wouldn't be too pretty, now, would it?"

"John . . ."

John looked down at his hand. He tumbled his keys back and forth from his fingers to his palm. He started for the back of the Mustang. The keys slid from him and chimed against the asphalt.

The sheriff put his light on them. "Go ahead. Pick 'em up."

John bent. As his fingers brushed the ground he sprang forward, head down, the sheriff's gut for a target.

Sheriff Potter was on the far side of being middle-aged, and calling him fat was being kind. But he wasn't slow. He sidestepped, and dropped a fist into the side of John's head. In the same motion he did a quick draw with his gun. John looked up and got a faceful of revolver.

"Is that the way you want it, boy? A bullet in the head in the middle of the desert? Ends like that and you won't be able to spend a dime of that blood money."

Grace jerked straight up in her seat. She shot a finger out at John. "He killed Jake, Sheriff. I couldn't stop him."

John's head swung around, hand cupped to his swelling face. "You bitch!"

"He made me come with him. He told me if I said a word, he would kill me."

Sheriff Potter spread his arms the way a referee comes between clutching boxers. "Shut up! The both of you. Ain't neither of you long on smarts." Down at John: "Especially you, boy. Don't you think I had my eye on you since first you rolled up into town? You smell like trouble. Stink of it like a ripe cesspool."

Dizzy, John took a few extra steps up to his feet. "I didn't do anything."

"Killing Jake McKenna's got to amount to something.

He wasn't much of a man, but, well . . . hell, try explaining that to a jury. And don't tell me you didn't kill him 'cause I was there when you did it."

Grace got all pathetic. "Sheriff Potter, please. I can't go to jail. I didn't want any part of it."

"You liar! You wanted him dead! You seduced me into killing him!"

Raising up in her seat, Grace got hard. "I told you not to fucking yell at me!"

"For the love of God, would you two give it a rest?" The sheriff's head made a slow swing from side to side. "In all my years I have never seen anything so pitiful. How far did you think you were going to get with this? Neither of you can wait to slit the other's throat." He holstered his gun. "Now use what smarts you got. If I was going to bust you, would I have waited until after you killed Jake?"

John and Grace thought, figured, and weighed the new rules of the game.

Grace came to the obvious. "What do you want?"

"Same thing you want. I want to be out of Sierra, to be able to do as I please. But that takes money."

"That's what this is about?" John asked. "Blackmail? You picked the wrong people. We don't have any money."

"Sure you do. Everybody in town knows about the money Jake kept hid in the house. It's a wonder the missus here just got round to killing him. Not for lack of trying."

That came at John fast and strong. He staggered with the blow.

The sheriff laughed, and the laugh rippled across his gut. "What'd you think? That you were the first man to drift through this town that she came onto? Not by a long shot. You're just the dumbest. How much you get?"

STRAY DOGS

John hesitated. "Thirty thousand."

Sheriff Potter's head dropped and he rubbed the back of his neck. "You're not passing these tests, boy. If I can't trust you, I'm gonna have to arrest you. I know Jake had more than thirty thousand dollars."

From the Mustang Grace hissed, "Don't tell him anything. He can't do this."

"I can't? You're out in the desert, all alone with a body in your trunk? And what with those two murders you committed back in town? You're like a mad dog."

"John, what the hell is he talking about?"

"Two men in a silver Lincoln." The sheriff smiled. "Hell, boy, I know they was armed, but you didn't have to gun them down like that. You're a mad dog, yes you are."

"Oh, Jesus . . . You killed them! You can't pin that on me!"

"Yeah, I killed them. But the way I've got things worked? You'll swing just the same."

"You son-of-a-bitch!"

"You can't hardly blame me, can you? I couldn't let anything happen to you. Not when you was about to do me a great big favor. Face it, boy. I can fuck you forty ways before breakfast. Now . . . how much money did you get?"

There wasn't much way around things, and John didn't even try to find one. "One hundred thousand dollars. A little more."

"Damn you!" Grace screamed. "He can't prove anything. What did you tell him for?"

"Yeah, maybe I should've kept my mouth shut so I could go to a hanging alone. That'd work out for you nice, wouldn't it?"

Sheriff Potter let out a deep, tired breath. "Nobody's

155

gonna hang. We're all gonna walk away with our pockets full. Now, I'm not a greedy man, I just want a little something for my troubles. One hundred thousand dollars. Split that three ways, it comes to about thirty-three thousand. Give or take."

"And you're taking," John noted.

The sheriff's face moved, his features distorted and grotesque in the Mustang's headlights.

Grace's voice cut like a razor. "All he's got is talk. He's got nothing on us. He let you kill Jake."

John came back strong. "Not me. Us."

"It doesn't matter. He was there and he let it happen. He can't take us in."

"Give him the money, Grace."

In a weak gasp Grace asked, "What?"

"You heard me. Count it out."

"He can't prove anything," she pleaded. "He can't turn us in."

"He can turn us in, he can kill us, he can do whatever he wants. I don't know about you, but my life's worth thirty thousand dollars."

Sheriff Potter to John: "Thirty-three thousand."

John to Grace: "Count it out."

The sheriff pulled a canvas bag from the small of his back and tossed it to the Mustang. "There you go, Mrs. McKenna. Just load it in there."

"John—"

"Do it, Grace!"

The sheriff turned back to John. He wore a self-satisfied smile, big and wide. "That wasn't so bad. What's thirty-some thousand dollars to rich folk like yourselves? It didn't hurt a bit."

Grace's voice came floating over from the Mustang, sweetly, like a whiff of jasmine in the summer air. "Sheriff Potter."

The sheriff turned and looked full on into Jake's .45. He snapped back a hand for his gun. For an older, overweight man, Sheriff Potter was quick.

But not near quick enough.

Grace jerked the trigger: a click, a roar, a white flash. The sheriff's stomach coughed and spat a stream of blood. He staggered backward, to the ground, and sat there clutching at the red river that flowed from his gut.

"Come on," Grace yelled at John.

John didn't move. He stood and stared, as dazed as the sheriff; a stain of blood soaking its way across his shirt. It was almost as easy to see the life draining from him.

"Dammit! Get in the car!"

John walked backward, stumbled, eyes locked on Sheriff Potter, who sat, without making a sound, dying. He fell into the car, fumbled the key into the ignition, and peeled out.

He looked back over his shoulder. He looked back at the sheriff, in the middle of the road, lit up by the headlights of his police car, his face bewildered.

John thought, You think you see it coming, but you don't. You think you got things worked, but things change. It don't matter how much you know, 'cause no matter how much you think you're hip to it, you can't know it all. Nobody can. And it's what you don't know, that's what kills you. That's how it happened for Jake. That's how it happened for Sheriff Potter. Richie and his goon friend, too. And the same could happen for him. The very same. There was so goddamn much John didn't know.

He turned to Grace. "What the hell did you do?"

"I shot him." Her voice came from far away.

"You killed him!"

"He was going to take the money."

"Thirty thousand, that's all. We would have been free and clear. You didn't have to kill him!"

"It's our money. He had no right to take it."

John looked at Grace. Not with lust, or desire, or some other animal urge that he'd been carrying around for the last twenty-four hours. He truly looked at her. Maybe for the first time. What he saw was dark, and ugly, and full of rage, and it frightened him. He didn't know, but he figured what he saw had always been there, he'd just been too simple to see it. Things came plain to him now.

"You're crazy, you know that, Grace? You're fucked in the head."

"Drive," she said.

John kept up the stare.

"Just drive!"

The Mustang rode on. Alone.

T here was a hurt in John's back. The Mustang's seats weren't much for sleeping, what little sleeping he did. He sat, legs dangling from the open door. The car was parked not too many yards from the edge of a plateau that was a long way from anywhere. Anything. Dull chatter from the car radio filled up the emptiness.

John lifted his head from his hands and looked over at Grace. She lay back in the passenger seat, eyes closed. Asleep. Maybe.

Grace had changed the previous night on that desolate road. A pulled trigger, a fatal shot, a split second, and she had evolved into something John hardly recognized. Or maybe, he thought, she had just gone back to what she had always been.

John dropped his face again into his hands. The sun began to slow-cook the back of his neck. He listened to the radio.

". . . Nobody's sure where the biker was heading so fast, but the way he hit the semi-truck he won't be getting there now. Hey, I got area weather. It's gonna be hot, hot, hot! Just like yesterday. Just like every day. Some surprise, huh? Weatherman says it's going to top one hundred again, so if you have to go outside, don't.

"Here's news from around the area. Over in Sierra, that sleepy little town was rocked by a series of murders that included the local sheriff among the victims. Authorities say they haven't made any arrests, but they have leads, and hope to bring in suspects within—"

John twisted the key, killing the alternator and the radio with it.

Grace's eyelids lifted.

"Jesus, Grace, did you have to kill him?"

"You still on that? He was going to—"

"I know. He was going to take the fucking money."

She lifted a hand and brushed it against John's neck. "You're tense. What are you all uptight about?"

John's eyes fell along Grace, over her tits and stomach, to her waist. Jake's automatic was tucked in the front of her pants. Her lips curled and she showed teeth. "Is that what's bothering you?"

Grace stood and stretched and casually walked round the front of the car to John. Running his tongue over his lips, he raised up, and met her.

Grace said: "You think now that Jake's dead, there's all that money there, and I don't really need your services any-more, I might just sneak up behind you and . . ."

She pointed a finger at John, then gave it a quick recoil. "That what got you down?" She gave a fucked-up laugh.

John missed the funny.

Grace's arms dropped to her side and hung naturally.

She and John stood facing each other, several feet apart, like a pair of gunfighters waiting for the last chime of the noon bell. Only, Grace was at a slight advantage, actually having a weapon.

"Is that the kind of girl you think I am? What can I do to make you relax?"

"You could give me the gun."

Her smile got bigger and showed more teeth; white like ivory in the snow. "Why don't we just finish what we started?"

"Why don't we?" He went slowly to the trunk of the car. Already cracked, he lifted it all the way open. Flies buzzed, and a stiff, sickly stench hit him in the face, slapping back his head. "Jesus, Jake. You need a bath."

John leaned into the trunk and got a grip on the body. Grace came up behind him. He couldn't see her, but he felt her just as he'd feel an unseen insect crawling on exposed flesh. John pulled at Jake. Death hadn't made him any lighter, just stiffer. He pulled again. Jake refused to go anywhere.

Without looking back, John said, "Give me a hand."

Grace didn't move.

"Are we going to dump him or not?"

A shadow cut across John as Grace came around. She went to the opposite end of the body and took hold.

John tightened his grip. "On three. Ready?"

Grace filled her hands with Jake's pant legs and nodded. "One, two—"

Low and fast and true, John swung his fist. It smashed into Grace's face just below the nose. A warm spray of blood soaked against his knuckles.

The blow lifted Grace from her feet. She traveled

backward, arms and legs flailing like a discarded rag doll. Her back took the fall, sending up a cloud of dust as it slapped the ground. She lay there, dazed and bleeding.

John went to her and slipped the gun from her waistband. He stood over her and watched her eyes slide back into place.

She put fingers to her lips. They came back bloody.

Grace laughed.

It was the kind of wild, crazed laugh that got people sent away to a nice place in the countryside where everyone was real polite to you as long as you didn't try to go beyond the chain-link fence.

"You hit me. You hit a woman. Didn't your mama ever teach you anything?" She saw the gun in John's hand. All of a sudden things weren't so funny anymore. "Well?"

John looked down at her. For a second he caught a flash of Sheriff Potter sitting in the middle of the road. The gun got real cold and heavy to his arm. He stuffed it in his waistband.

"Well, nothing," he said.

"Now what?"

"Now we dump the body, split the money, then you're on your own."

Grace stuttered, like it took her a second to get the idea. "But you said we could be together."

"Are you kidding? I'm not going down with you for killing a cop."

"What difference does it make? You killed Jake."

"*We* killed Jake. And it's a big difference. You kill an old man, that's one thing. Nobody cares about an old man. You kill a cop and they never stop looking for you. Never."

John walked to the Mustang, put his hands on the hood, and propped himself up.

"Sheriff Potter was a crooked bastard. He would have killed us if we gave him the chance."

"The police don't know that. And it's the kind of thing that's hard to explain when you've got a noose around your neck." He struggled with a couple of ideas, a couple of different ways to play things, but there was really only one way to go from here. "I'll take you to California. If we can make it that far. After that, I'm cutting you loose."

She went to him; arms around his waist, head to his chest. "But I want to stay with you."

Her voice was so sweet John got sick on it. "Why? So when the cops catch up with us you can try to sell me out again?" Pulling himself free, he brushed her aside, a bothersome fly. "You take your half of the money and run. You might want to try Mexico. With all that dough you'll live like a queen." John crossed round for the trunk.

Grace, kind of pouty like a high-school girl trying to get her way: "I don't want to go to Mexico. I want to be with you. Don't you think I care about you?"

John stopped. He turned back to her. "I think you're a lying, backstabbing bitch. But it's nice to know you care." He went for the body.

John tore a beer from a six-pack, and shoved it in Jake's pocket. Taking him under the arms, he pulled the dead man up from the trunk and dragged the body toward the plateau's edge.

"Poor old Jake. Had a fight with the wife, put down a few too many drinks, wandered into the desert, and fell off a cliff. You should have been more careful."

At the lip of the plateau John stood the body up and

turned it to face him. Holding Jake by the shoulders, John spoke to the dead man as if he were a dear friend about to walk out the door.

"Well, Jake. This is where we part company." Leaning close to whisper: "You should have just let me go into the bedroom. I would have given it to her. You or Grace; it didn't make a damn bit of difference which of you got dead to me. Now look at yourself. Oh, well. See ya, lad, and thanks for the loan."

John spread his hands. The body stood for a moment, then lost its balance and tumbled backward off the ledge. It made one perfect flip—graceful as an Olympic diver—then plunged straight into the ground. Jake nailed it. Degree of difficulty 2.0.

John looked down after the body. "Now all we have to do is—"

He turned. Grace was right behind him. Startled, he took a step back. His foot came down on air. The last thing he saw was Grace's hands at his chest. Maybe she was pushing him, maybe she was grabbing for him. The bitch of it, he thought as he went back off the ledge into the big, wide, empty sky, is that he would never know.

Hell. This time John might just have made it. It was hot enough to be hell. And it hurt like hell. Like the way he thought hell is supposed to hurt, anyway. But it was the kind of mortal hurt that told John he was still alive. He opened his eyes. Jake stared back at him.

Grace's voice came down from the mountain. "John . . . ? John . . . !"

"Grace!" He tried to sit up. A handful of razors raced

along the length of his right leg and back down again. John screamed accordingly.

"Are you all right?" Grace yelled down.

"I think I busted my leg."

"Can you climb back up?"

Putting a hand to the rock face, John tried to pull himself to his feet. The razors came back. "I can't make it, Grace. Grace?"

Nothing.

"Grace!"

"I'm here."

"Grace, listen to me. In the trunk of the car is a rope. It ought to reach down here. Get it, throw it down to me, and I'll climb up."

Grace ran back to the Mustang. The rope sat prominently in the open trunk. She shot a hand out, but it froze in the air. Thoughts came at her quick. She slammed the trunk closed. Rounding the car, Grace slid behind the wheel, her hand fumbled at the ignition. Real quick, panic was on her before she even knew why. Her fingers had nothing to grab. No key.

Shit!

Fast out of the car and back to the ridge. She leaned over the side and yelled down.

"John! Can you hear me? Are you still there?"

"Where the hell am I going to go?"

"John, the keys; you have to throw them up to me."

With all the pain in the world, John managed a hand into his pocket and worked free the keys. He leaned back and cocked his arm. It would be a good throw up to Grace, but not one he couldn't make. Something, like a bad itch, stopped him before he even tried.

"John, throw me the keys." Grace lay on the edge of the plateau and looked down.

"What for?"

"The trunk. It's locked."

"It's not locked. I left it open when I took out Jake's body."

"It's . . . it's locked."

"You closed it, didn't you, Grace?"

"I was going to back the car to the ridge and pull you up." She came back quick with that, just like she'd been quick with comebacks before. Calm and cool. Honest and real. If John hadn't known Grace better, he just might have believed her.

"Bullshit!" The word echoed, and a dozen Johns screamed at Grace. "You were going to drive off and leave me here."

"No. I swear it."

"And you're not one to lie, are you, Grace?"

"Throw me the keys, and I'll pull you up."

"Why don't you come down and get them so I can wring your little throat."

Grace rolled onto her back. She blocked out the sun with her hand and stared up into the endless blue sky. Quiet, perfect, beautiful. Hot. She rolled back onto her stomach and yelled down at John.

"If you don't throw me the keys, I'll just walk away. I'll take the money and walk away and leave you here."

"Walk to where, Grace? We're fifty miles to the closest town. It'll be over a hundred degrees today. How far do you think you're going to get?"

"Someone will find me."

A big, fat laugh: "Yeah, they'll find you. Dried up, and twice dead."

"You idiot! You'll kill us both!"

"At least I'll have company when I die." A quick look to the body next to him. "Ain't that right, Jake?"

"For Christ sake, John!" Grace's voice came frightened and pathetic. "Throw me the keys!"

"What do you say, Jake? Should we trust her?" Anything Jake had to say he kept to himself. That was enough for John. "I didn't think so."

"Fuck you!" Grace's voice came down on John like a storm. "Do you hear me? Fuck you! John . . . ? John . . . !"

Grace waited for an answer, some kind of response.

Nothing.

She sat there in the sun.

After a while she went back to the Mustang, slung the one hundred thousand dollars over her shoulder, and headed out into the desert.

Someone will find me, she kept telling herself. Someone will find me.

Grace wiped the sweat from her forehead.

John got as comfortable as the rocks and his broken leg would allow. He popped open the beer and raised it in a toast.

"Here's to you, Jake. A friend to the end." He washed the words down with a healthy swig. It was warm, but a good buzz would help keep down the pain in his leg. For a little while, anyway. "And to Grace. What a woman. What a fucking woman."

Jake had nothing to add to that.

John stared at his dead friend, his face a death mask of confusion. He thought of Sheriff Potter, who wore the same look when he died. John was like them, in a way; in the end he hadn't seen death coming. That's where the confusion came from, as if in the very last second of life Jake and the sheriff had tried desperately to piece together how things could turn so horribly bad.

But for John it had been there all the time, right in front of him; the object of his own destruction. But it looked so good and felt so right and fucked so well he hadn't even noticed the ax had begun to fall. Or worse yet, maybe he had seen it, but it fucked so well he just didn't want to get out of the way.

At least, John consoled himself, unlike Jake and Sheriff Potter, he had time—hours, days maybe—to figure things out, to see where it all went wrong. At least when he died he wouldn't look so perplexed.

John wondered how Grace would look when they found her.